Roopesh Kumar is a contemporary Indian author. He was born on 15th August in New Delhi, India, and completed his degree from University of Delhi. After completing his degree, he took a break from study to gain some real work experience and focus on writing. He has worked with some reputed organizations such as IBM and Aon Hewitt.

This is his second novel which he took more than three years to write. His debut novel *I'm An Average Looking Boy...will you be my girl friend?* was a huge success and became a national bestselling novel. He lives in New Delhi, likes travelling, watches Hindi movies during leisure time, and has a keen interest in reading.

For more updates, like his Facebook page @iroopeshkumar

Or follow him on Twitter and Instagram @iroopeshkumar

POTENTIAL BOYFRIEND

ROOPESH KUMAR

Pengo

Publications India

Pengo Publications India
New Delhi 110078
Info.pengopublications@gmail.com

First published by Pengo Publications India

ISBN: 9788193225349

Printed and bound in India.

To—the God we can see, touch and feel—Children

PROLOGUE

'Oh SHITTTT,' I screamed out. I fell on my face between the two berths. I was in the third coach of Janshatabdi train—Delhi to Chandigarh. And as soon as I reached near my berth, I didn't know how my right leg slipped and the very next moment I was lying straight on the train floor. I lifted my head and saw a guy sitting on my right, opposite to my berth. He had held his hands on the window grill, peeping outside. I thought he would turn to me and offer his hand to help me get up. But he didn't pay any heed and kept peeping outside, unfazed with the mess around him. As if nothing happened there. And then I heard a few children clapping and chuckling behind. I felt a twinge on my left cheekbone.

Well, somehow, I got up and plonked myself on my berth, getting rid of my backpacks immediately. I looked at those children. They were still giggling and nudging each other, looking at me sideways. I frowned at them and they hid behind each other. They stopped giggling.

Hastily, I pulled out my mobile from the jeans pocket and peered into the screen to check if I had got any cut or a swollen face. It seemed normal, but pained badly.

And then, suddenly, I saw a girl getting down from the upper berth through the terrible ladder attached there. I looked up at her. Abruptly, my pain got relegated. I pushed my mobile back into my pocket quickly and craned my neck forward.

She wore a black pair of Jeggings and a white crop-top. Slim and fair in appearance. It took me just a few seconds to recognize all this. I couldn't look at her face as her beautiful hair hid that. I didn't care. I had already got reasons to call her beautiful.

She jumped as soon as her leg touched the last uncomfortable metal rod of the ladder. And that was the very first time I felt these ladders to climb up to the upper berths in trains are really terrible. These should be replaced with some new comfortable ladders immediately. As immediately as she comes back and tries to climb up to her berth again.

Well, I couldn't resist myself looking at her walking away. Probably, she was going to the washroom.

'BOOTY-FULL. Not it?' Suddenly, I heard this voice. It came from the guy sitting opposite to my berth.

Surprised, I gazed at him, mouth open. He was smiling weirdly. He was tall, about three inches above me—5'11. Black hair, deep eyes, thin and elongated nose, and fair skin, he had got nice features. But it seemed, his *No-Shave-November* had followed for the whole year, he hadn't shaved for months. He also looked fragile underneath his full sleeves olive-round-neck-t-shirt. Messy hair and dirty clothes. But, Levi's denim, Nike sneakers and a fancy watch in hand stopped me to consider him a homeless beggar. He looked like someone in his thirties. I guessed.

'Isn't she beautiful?' he said before I could respond to him. I shut my mouth. And I got his *booty-full*. Crap!

I shook my head up, dilating the size of my pupils. As if asking 'What the hell are you talking about, man?'

'I SAW YOU OGLING AT HER ASS,' he said, grinning. It turned my face red. Suddenly, a feeling of embarrassment ran through my blood. I wondered how brazenly he could say that.

So what? You expect me to stare at your ass? You moron! I thought to say.

'EXCUSE… ME???' I blurted out. I made my face as shocked as possible. I took a deep breath and wondered what to say next. Well, I continued, 'No, I'm not… I mean you're mistaken.'

I turned my face away and decided to ignore him before he could spew out anything else. I moved back in my berth and started looking outside the window, even when it was dark outside. After a few seconds, unwillingly, I squinted at him. He was still looking at me, smiling weirdly.

'What's wrong with you, dude?' I murmured to myself. You can't just sit idly knowing someone is staring at you constantly. I pulled my bag near, unzipped it and took out a novel that I was reading in those days. It takes me days to complete a novel. Well, I kept it close to my face to avoid any eye contact with him. After some time I peeped out of my novel to look at him. He was still looking at me. Weird smile on his face irritated me the most.

Fuck man! Are you a gay? Look, I don't have any problem if you're one, but I'm sure I'm not. So, leave me alone, you asshole, leave me alone, I thought to shout. But I didn't. I hid my face behind the novel. I went back to reading. And for a while, I just kept reading until that girl came back. I saw her climbing up to her berth. After looking at her for a few seconds I realized girls look extra attractive in crop-tops.

Well, then I looked at that guy, he was already staring at me. As expected. Our eyes met. Abruptly, I turned my gaze away and moved my head around, trying to act like I wasn't looking at the girl.

'You know what? I used to be more like you in your age,' he said, grinning as if he had said something very pleasing to my ears and I would just get up and run to hug him.

More like me? Means you used to ogle at girls' ass? But dude, I'm not an eve-teaser like you look. You, poor old ass. Huh, I thought.

I hunted for words. So, I just faked a smile at him.

And suddenly, he got up, came to my berth and sat near. Now, it scared me a little. I slipped in my berth close to the window, maintaining as much distance as possible. I used my bag as a barrier between us.

'You reminded me of my old days.'

I shook my head. I wondered what I did to remind him of his fucking old days. I could say sorry if he wanted.

'What's your name?' he asked.

'R...Roopesh. I'm Roopesh Kumar,' I said, hesitantly. Dark circles beneath his eyes scared me. I wanted to offer him my goggles. But I didn't. I had borrowed them from one of my friends.

'What's your name?' I asked that he could say something instead of smiling weirdly.

'I'm Vardan...Vardan Awasthi,' he paused for a while and continued, 'So, going to Chandigarh?'

'No, Ambala, to attend a marriage,' I said, adding, 'You're going to Chandigarh?'

He nodded. I didn't ask why he was going to Chandigarh. I didn't care.

Meanwhile, I kept that novel beside, unzipped my bag and took out the chocolate cake I had bought from Rajiv Chowk metro station. I felt as if mice were dancing inside my stomach. I unwrapped that and offered it to my uninvited guest. I gulped that chocolate cake in one go as soon as he refused my offer.

'How old are you?' I mumbled, running my jaw. I don't know what made me to ask this question suddenly. Maybe the mismatch between the way he looked and behaved.

'Twenty Seven,' he acknowledged.

'WHATTT?' I shouted in shock as if he had said he was just a ten-year-old.

Dude, you look too poor to be called twenty seven, I thought.

'What happened?'

'No, nothing. You… you look, I mean…sorry, you don't look like twenty seven. Even you look like someone in his thirties,' I said, tentatively.

'LOVE MADE ME LOOK LIKE THIS,' he said laughingly. For the first time I noticed an intense gaze in his deep eyes. I slowed down grinding the cake inside my mouth. You can't keep on enjoying your food when someone suddenly mentions something unusual. Even if it's chocolate cake. I wondered what to say next.

'Well, how old are you? Twenty or twenty one?' he added.

I gestured to answer and then suddenly the train stopped with a buzzing noise. Our first stop or the next station had arrived.

'I'm going to have tea. Would you like to join?' I said.

'Sure.'

He chose to have tea only. I ordered a bread-pakoda too. We came back to our respective berths with tea cups in our hands. I pushed my bag under my berth before sitting. We had our first few sips of tea in silence. Later, I went on reading my novel again. I opened it holding in my left hand and started reading, the cup of tea in my right hand.

I had read a few lines before Vardan interrupted. Yet again.

'So, you read novels?'

'No, this is my new hobby. And I'm in love with it,' I exclaimed. You love people talk about something you have recently added to your hobby. I threw out empty cup of tea through the window.

'It seems a love story book?'

'Yeah, these days I'm reading love stories. But, I don't like sad endings. My last novel had a very sad-ending. It ruined my mood for a few weeks. I hated that. Love stories should have happy endings. At least in books. No?' I paused to look at him. He had turned quiet. His gaze had fallen down. I waited for him to respond. But he kept looking down.

I'm sorry if I said anything wrong, I wanted to say. But I couldn't.

He looked up at me, sensing the sudden silence there. Abruptly, he brought a smile on his face. Perhaps, a fake one.

'Yes, it should,' he said, smirking. His head trembled. And then he grew silent. He turned his gaze away and peeped out through the window. I went back to reading.

After some time I looked at my watch. It said 10 pm.

'It's dinner time,' I mumbled to myself. I looked at him. He was lying in his berth. I faced his back.

'Hey, you slept? How about the dinner?' I called him loudly.

He turned his face. 'I'm waiting for the train to stop.' The very first sentence he said without smiling. I appreciated that.

'You don't need to. I have brought enough Gobhi ke parathe. And I don't mind sharing,' I said, pulling my bag out. And the next moment we were having parathe with pickle in my berth.

We finished our dinner and talked for a while. Later, I decided to sleep. Next day I had to be at a wedding house and wouldn't get any opportunity to take a nap even. I lay down and tried to sleep.

Although, I started thinking about Vardan. His brazen encounter, a constant smile on his face, the way he looked and his sudden expression change on the topic of love. Eccentric.

Why did he say 'love made me look like this?' I thought. And he just agreed he looked weird? Whatever. I must sleep now.

I changed my side, stretched my legs straight, closed my eyes, and tried to sleep. However, you just can't sleep if something is bothering you inside. I tried my best to sleep and not to think about him. But half an hour later, I realized I wasn't able to sleep.

Had someone betrayed him? His girlfriend slept with someone else? He loved someone who eloped with some other guy? His girlfriend met with an accident? Is she dead? Random questions popped up.

All of a sudden, I got up and sat in my berth. I looked at him. He was lying straight. He had covered his eyes with his right hand on his head. I wondered if he had slept.

'You didn't sleep yet?' suddenly, he said, still lying straight and his hand still covering his face. So, he was acting asleep.

'No. I'm not feeling sleepy.'

'Why? What happened?' he asked, turning towards me.

'What's your story?' I asked. And abruptly, he got up. He shook his head. Surprisingly.

'Yes, I want to know what your story is. Why did you say love made you look like this? Even why did you grow silent while talking about love stories?' I fired questions at him.

'Suddenly?'

'Not actually. It's been bothering me since you said that thing.'

'Hmmm,'

'What?'

'You really want to know?' he said.

'Fuck really. I'm curious to know if you feel comfortable sharing with me,' I shrugged my shoulders, sounding nosy.

After thinking for a few seconds, he nodded.

Without wasting time, I went to his berth and sat cross-legged, right opposite to him.

'Where do I start from?'

'Where every story starts,' I exclaimed.

'When we first met?'

'I want it all. Start with something so that I can know you better.'

1.

'WHAT THE FUCK? Vardan...? You scared the shit out of me,' she screamed, gasping and squashing her right chest. I smirked, glancing at her.

I had just pushed the brake of my car in front of my house. It had stopped before the tyres were dragged on the neat and clean Jet-black road, emitting a loud squeal. I drove an Audi and you can't get the real feeling of driving an Audi until you push the power brake hard at a speed of eighty.

Well, I was with my girlfriend Saumya, Saumya Chadha. MY NEW GIRLFRIEND at that time. That day, my parents were out of town. So, I had brought her to my place—101 Aurangzeb-road, just right beside Delhi's famous business tycoon Somani's house.

'You okay?' I said, grinning wickedly. I unlocked my seat belt and helped her to unlock hers. I picked up my mobile and wallet.

'OKAY??? See, my heart is beating fast. Sitting in your car means endangering your life, huh,' she said, eying towards her hand on chest and still trying to recover the shock.

'See, that's my house,' I pointed towards my house, without bothering much about her concern. She peeped out of the car window. I got out of the car. She followed.

'Wow!!! This is where you live?' she was stunned. She lifted her sunglasses over her forehead with mouth wide open, while placing her right hand beneath her chin. I liked her reaction though.

Actually, my house wasn't just a regular house. It was a massive mansion. My father was one of Delhi's richest businessmen. I was his only child. And this helped me to get girlfriends so easily.

I shrugged my shoulders. She grabbed my arm and smiled. We walked towards my house. I was getting excited with every step I was taking with her. No one was home. I had already asked our maid and domestic help not to come that day. Saumya and I were going to be alone for the first time. And even this mere thought was enough to drive me crazy. My whole body was tingling in fantasies of us being together as we walked towards the main door of my house. We stepped inside.

'It's huge, Vardan… beautiful house,' she exclaimed as soon as she entered and looked around, her hands cupping her face , eyes wide open. I slammed the door shut behind us. I locked it. Her exhilaration was making me giggle inside.

'Not more beautiful than you,' I said, standing behind her. At First, I gestured to hug her from behind but then paused as I didn't want to look desperate.

'Whatever… I love you, Vardan,' she said, still moving her head around, standing in the middle of the living room. She acted like a nine-year-old who was left in a huge toy shop. Although, I was ready to buy her the best possible toy.

I pulled her towards me and abruptly, she fell into my arms. I grabbed and held her.

'I know, baby. That's why you're here, with me…ALONE,' I said, emphasizing the last word. She blushed. I found that blush adorable.

'So, you don't even offer your guests water?' she said, grinning and constantly blinking her eyes. . I let her go off my grip.

'Sorry, I will get you some water,' I said and ran towards the kitchen, took out a water bottle from the fridge and came back running.

I gulped some water and then offered her the bottle. I showed her my house till she emptied the water bottle. She seemed really thirsty. Not more than me though.

'You want to have something?' I asked. 'Okay, wait. Let me bring something for you,' I added before she could respond. Again, I ran back to the kitchen and looked for some food options there. Neither had I wanted to waste any time in cooking, nor did I know how to cook. I picked a tray and filled it with whatever I found in the kitchen—Haldiram Khatta Meetha Namkeen, dry fruits, cookies, brown bread, jam, sweets and fruits. It seemed like a pile of things. Edible things.

We sat on the sofa and talked. Well, she talked. I just kept looking at her. I just sat near, discerning the every bit of her. She was fair, slim and voluptuous. She wore a red deep neck tank top and black skirt—which hardly covered her half thighs. I liked that skirt. Her silky soft hair kept falling on her face while talking. That hid her cleavage. I wanted to chop half of her hair and tie the remaining behind, so that it wouldn't fall near her neck. But I didn't. I just kept staring at her.

As she sat near me, I kept imagining myself taking her clothes off. It turned me on so badly. Clung in her tank top and her bare legs didn't allow me to concentrate on her nonstop banter.

2.

I moved myself closer to her, keeping my left hand around her shoulder. I stroked my fingers behind her neck, gently.

'It's tickling, Vardan,' she giggled loudly. I didn't stop. Even I slid my hand in her tee from behind. I felt her soft skin. My hand reached her bra strap. I grabbed and held her in my arms, completely ignoring what she was talking about. Probably, I had not brought her there to sit and talk.

'What are you doing, Vardan?' she said, laughingly. I didn't appreciate her laugh at that moment. I leaned forward to kiss her. I kissed on her neck and moved towards her lips. And at the last moment she moved her face away, towards the wall opposite to the sofa we were lying on, and I ended up kissing my sofa, upholstered in expensive silk. I hated that fancy sofa. Money cannot buy all the happiness, I just felt.

'Hey, beautiful scenery,' she exclaimed. She extracted herself from my grip, got up and moved towards the wall. She stood there and admiring that scenery, as if a serious art lover was standing in an exhibition. There was a horse in the picture, running to save her life from the lion chasing behind. I imagined that lion to peep out of the picture and scare her so that she could throw herself back to me and hide in my arms. But nothing happened like that. And I came to know how useless that costly scenery was.

Useless animal! You'll never be able to catch that horse, I thought. I wanted to scream this. But I didn't. I felt like taking a hammer and breaking that scenery into pieces. I stopped, thinking about all the expenses my father had to bear buying it.

I stood up and walked to her. I hugged her from behind, my chin dug deep into her right shoulder.

'Dad wasted twenty thousand pounds to bring this home. This painting is painted by late George Stubbs and was auctioned highest by my father last year in a London exhibition,' I mumbled, kissing on her neck.

'TWENTY THOUSAND POUNDS??? God …! Your father is also an art lover,' she murmured, more to herself. I could still hear her.

'Leave this! Well, come, I will show you my room,' I said. I grabbed her arm and we walked towards my room.

I slammed the door shut behind us as soon as she entered my room. She went to the wall lined with my pictures.

'These are your pictures?' she said, pointing at one of my childhood pictures. I was wearing a pink shirt and white jeans in that picture. I looked very innocent in that picture, totally opposite from the current day.

After inspecting all my pictures lined on the wall, she picked up a photo frame from the bed table and sat on my bed. I followed her from wall to my bed. I was getting tired of following her here and there. But, I wanted to appreciate her for going towards the bed.

'This is your mother?' she said, showing me the picture. The picture was of my mother. She was smiling, with a *dupatta* over her head. I wanted to pull that *dupatta* down till her eyes.

'Yes,' I said and snatched it from her hand. I placed it inside the drawer. 'She won't look at us now,' I said and grabbed her. We fell on the bed. I was on her. I tried to kiss her.

She kept her hands on her lips. 'What's going on?' she mouthed.

'Nothing. A boyfriend is trying to kiss his girlfriend,' I said, throwing her hands away. And the very next moment my lips met with hers. First I kissed her lower lip. After a few seconds she started responding. She started moving her hands softly through my bristle. It drove me crazy. Then I didn't stop. I started kissing her lips like anything. So did she. We kept kissing for next few minutes. We stopped to take some oxygen, gasping. She was good at kissing. I must admit.

I continued to kiss her. I kissed on her head, on her eyes, on her cheeks and then on her neck. She sighed when I kissed behind her right ear. I came down her neck, kissing. I shoved my head in her cleavage. My right hand on her breast and left slid under her skirt, caressing her soft thighs. She moaned loudly as soon as my hand touched there. I liked her moaning.

We sat up. I removed my shirt and pulled up her top, eying her to take that off. She lifted her hands up instead and I removed her top. We lay down again. I took my hands behind and unhooked her pink bra. She immediately held her bra keeping it on its place. She looked away, shyly. I started kissing on her neck and gently removed her hands from there. Now she was half naked in front of me. I paused to look at her for a while. I underwent millions of orgasm by seeing her half-naked body. I almost fainted.

'You're the most beautiful and the best girl I have ever met,' I exclaimed, holding her breasts and leaned on her. I kissed her for a while and she kissed on my chest.

'Vardan, It's enough for the day, I guess,' she mumbled.

'We have just started,' I whispered. I came down. Kissed on her navel when my hands stroked her thighs. She pressed my head with her hands. I giggled inside seeing her in action.

'SO, TODAY. FINALLY... YOU'RE GOING TO LOSE YOUR VIRGINITY, Vardan,' I murmured to myself, excitedly. I wanted to pat my shoulder. Finally, I was going to start a perfect relationship.

I stopped and tried to unhook her skirt. Suddenly, she sat up and caught my hands.

'No, Vardan. Enough for the day,' she said.

'Baby, we have just started. And love can never be enough, even when it feels amazing,' I whispered, touching her cheeks. She didn't respond. I successfully unhooked and removed her skirt. I kissed on her thighs for a while. And gestured to remove the last clothe on her body.

But she caught my hands and protested, 'Please, Vardan, don't.' She sat up again.

'What happened?' I mumbled, kissing on her legs. 'Aren't you enjoying it?'

'That's not the point, and please stop it now,' she said in a firm voice.

I sat up and shrugged my shoulders in disappointment.

'We can't have sex. Even I didn't want to do all this, now,'

'WHATTT? But why? Why? Why?' I was disappointed. A part of me said *it's not going to happen today as well. Your misery will follow some more. You're going to stay virgin, Vardan, virgin.*

I didn't want to believe that. I wanted to hit my head on the wall.

'Why…??? How can we do this so early?'

'But you said you love me?'

'Yes, I do. But…'

'What?'

'We have known each other just for a week,' she said. She stood up and looked around for her clothes. She was in her underwear only, standing in front of me. I wanted to pull her underwear down and go ahead. But I stopped as I didn't want to be called a molester or rapist.

I had met Saumya one week ago. We met in a marriage.

'But we're meeting for the fourth time? No? In our last three dates, I took you to Ambience mall for shopping, we went to Starbucks, and day before yesterday we had dinner at Indian Accent. So, I guess we have spent lots of time together in last one week. We have done a lot of talking. Moreover, we love each other,' I said, throwing my hands in air and looking at her.

'Yet, Vardan, it's too early. And even you haven't promised me for marriage yet,' she said, pulling her skirts up. I hated her doing so.

'Marriage?' I groaned. Even this word sent me into a state of shock. 'How can you even expect me to promise you for marriage this early?'

'Exactly, Vardan… EARLY. It's too early to discuss all this,' she said, adjusting her top. Her navel peeped out of her top. I wanted her to cover that too now.

It was enough for me to realize that I had to walk to the washroom. And I did the same. I stood up and walked towards the washroom.

'Where are you going?' she said.

To celebrate my thirteenth relationship failure. To release my frustration. Would you like to join the celebration? I thought to reply. But I didn't say anything. I went inside and shut the door.

She wasn't in room when I came back. I wore my shirt and came to the living room. She was sitting on the sofa, comfortably. I sat on the opposite sofa. I picked up my mobile from the table and started playing Candy Crush.

'Hey, are you angry?' she said.

'It's okay,' I said, without looking at her. I picked up few cashews and placed my legs on the table. She came and sat beside me.

'Baby, I'm sorry for ruining your mood,' she said. I didn't respond. I found Candy Crush more interesting than her. I hated her black skirt. I hated her legs. I hated her peeping navel. I hated her deep neck top showing her cleavage. And I hated her near me.

'Hey, aren't you listening to me? And are we going for a movie tomorrow?' she asked. We had a plan to go for a movie the next day.

I didn't respond. She repeated.

'We're not going anywhere,' I shouted when she repeated thrice. I stood up and sat on another sofa.

After a few minutes of silence,

'You don't want to talk to me anymore? Are we breaking up or something?' she shouted. I didn't respond. She repeated.

'Nice observation,' I mumbled. She glared at me. I didn't care.

'Well, we can discuss it later. Now, I'm getting late, please drop me that I can reach home on time,' she said, standing up and putting her bag in place.

I immediately faked a call, 'Hello, yes, Mom… oh, you're coming?' and after keeping the mobile on my ear for a while I acted as if disconnecting.

'See, my parents are coming. So, I won't be able to drop you. But, you can get an auto from outside. Else, you can also book a cab,' I said without looking at her and shrugged my shoulders.

She breathed heavily, pissed at me. I fell on my sofa, carefree.

'You can take some cashews to eat on the way.'

'Shove this in your ass,' she said and left fuming.

3.

Adithya jumped off the couch, few inches up in air and rolled down on the floor laughing when I told him about my last day's fling with Saumya. He tried to get up on his elbows but fell down again as he was laughing breathlessly. His white teeth popped out. I felt to break them in pieces.

'One more un-suck-sex-full breakup,' he said in between the laughs. I was lying on a sofa, legs stretched on table. I smiled grudgingly seeing him laugh endlessly.

'I always tell you, he is going to die a virgin,' said Sejal, grinning and looking at Adithya. He laughed some more. Sejal was ironing her clothes. I wanted to snatch the hot iron out of her hand and put that on Adithya's mouth.

'Vardan, remove your shoes before resting your legs on table, you know my maid is on leave for next two days,' suddenly, she shouted, in a protesting way. Instead I stretched my legs some more.

Adithya R Venkatesan and Sejal Ganguly were my best friends. That day, we were at Sejal's three-BHK apartment in New Friends Colony where she lived alone. Her parents lived in the USA. They filled her bank account and paid her credit card's bill whenever she complained that she missed them. She hated their ignorance towards her. She was like a tomboy. Tall, healthy, straight forward, and someone who plays guitar sitting on the floor, this is how she could be described the best. She was doing her Economics (H) from Lady Shri Ram College, DU. I knew her from school but I met Adithya in the first year of my college and we became best friends in a very short span of time. He was a huge fan of Rajnikant and couldn't even hear a single word against him. He was basically from Chennai and had come to Delhi for engineering. He lived in college hostel. He knew Sejal through me. That day I had called him to her place so that I could share my recent break up story with them.

'Were you guys all naked before she refused you to enter inside her?' asked Adithya in a sarcastic tone. He got up and sat beside me. Curiosity was sketched on his face. I frowned at him. I wanted to pull his hair. But didn't as he had very short hair.

'Stop fantasizing, you asshole,' I groaned.

'No, I'm just asking,' he mumbled, trying to hide his giggles behind his palm.

'Well, she was still wearing her last clothe,' I said, smirking wickedly at Adithya.

'Rubbish,' shouted Sejal. I along with Adithya laughed. She came and sat on the couch opposite to us. She had made omelet for her breakfast. She ate that with folk. Adithya leaned forward and grabbed a big piece of omelet in his fist.

'But, what if she loves you?' exclaimed Adithya, stroking his fingers on his chin, mouth filled with omelet.

'She loves me? Had that been the case, would she have really done everything that she did to me? She doesn't. Her chapter is close now.'

'Sex is not the destination of love,' Sejal interrupted.

'But sex takes you a step closer to love and relationship. Well, I don't want to fall into this love philosophy. I'm so done with this. At least, for the day,' I declared. I stood up and went to the kitchen. I took out an apple and a water bottle from the fridge and came back. I sat on another couch. Adithya was lost in his mobile. I bit a big piece of apple. White part of the apple reminded me of Saumya's soft milky skin. I hated that apple.

'You're never going to have a girl or a stable relationship this way,' she continued the argument. I continued to eat my apple. Adithya continued staring at his mobile screen.

'Yes, because I have got some useless friends like you,' I said, passing the water bottle to her.

She shrugged her shoulders, eyebrows raised.

'There are many hot chicks in LSR, but you never even introduce me to anyone,' I said, having the last apple bite.

'You don't even talk about this, you bastard!!! You forgot what you did with Anjali?' suddenly, she shouted. Her voice was loud enough to scare Adithya that he fell on the floor with his mobile.

I started laughing loudly as soon as I heard the name *Anjali*.

Anjali was one of my thirteen girlfriends. I had met her through Sejal as she was also from LSR College. After talking over the phone for one long week we had gone for a movie. And as soon as kiss scene appeared in the movie I felt like kissing her. So, I held her and tried to kiss on her lips which she didn't allow and I ended kissing on her cheeks. I made a face and watched the whole movie silently. Later, after the movie finished and we came out of the theatre, I tried to kiss her in my car and she denied again. After two or three unsuccessful attempts, I asked her to get out of my car. It was 10pm then. She started to protest and requested me to drop her home. I kept a condition before her that she needs to kiss me if she wants me to drop her. She agreed and then I kissed her the best I could have in the car. Later, she blocked my number and did the same on Facebook as soon as I dropped her home. Since then, Sejal taunts me with her name.

'Guys, I have had a break up very recently. Show some sympathy, instead of pulling my leg,' I stood up and shouted, trying to change the topic.

'You, *mother-fucker*!!! What the hell is wrong with you?' suddenly, Adithya screamed. I thought what kind of sympathy was that? He was glaring at me. I wondered what happened to him suddenly.

I shook my head, taking the water bottle from Sejal's hand. For next few minutes, he kept glaring at me. And I kept wondering what I had done to him, all of a sudden. I emptied the water bottle while he kept filling his eyes with anger.

'Why the hell have you commented on Jyothi's Facebook profile picture? *Looking hot... Nice ass*? Really?' he groaned. He threw a cushion at me.

Sejal started chuckling. I joined her. He kept fuming in anger.

'I thought this is what she wanted to show, as posing her back. And she also looked hot in that picture. I just meant to praise her,' I said, almost stammering. I tried to hide my smile. But I couldn't. Even I burst into laughter.

'*Bhenchod*!!! She is my cousin,' he shouted. His eyes were ready to fall out. He threw the TV remote towards me which I caught successfully. Sejal took a sigh of relief.

'Why, girls cannot look hot in your family?' I paused to grin, 'And don't over react, I wasn't flirting with her. It was just a comment, and even she has liked my comment,' I completed.

'You're such an asshole. I will ask her to block you, immediately,' he said, annoyingly. I continued laughing.

'Okay, sorry. I didn't know she was your cousin,' I said, holding him from behind.

'Fuck sorry, fuck the Facebook, and fuck yourself,' he shrieked and got rid of my grip. He got lost in his mobile once again as soon as I left him.

'You know what, I want a relationship, but I don't know why girls do this to me?' suddenly, I said, looking at Sejal. 'Look at this poor guy, even he isn't a virgin. I look much better than him. I drive an Audi while he roams with his girlfriend in auto, I take girls to the best restaurants in the city while he takes his girlfriend to roadside *dhaba* outside campus and moreover, I take girls for shopping while he asks his girlfriend to share the bill when they go out to eat. Yet I'm a virgin. Not fair, no?' I added, pointing at Adithya. He looked up and frowned at me. I passed a smile to him. He threw a cushion at me.

'He is a *potential boyfriend*,' said Sejal, brusquely.

'What?' I said. I sat on the corner of table, facing her.

'He is a potential boyfriend which you're not.'

'What does that mean? *Potential boyfriend*?' I said. I removed my shoes and sat on the table, straight and cross-legged, right opposite to her. I waited for her to respond as if she was going to give me the biggest advice of my life. My astrologer. Though, I really needed some advice. I needed to figure out what the fuck was going on in my life. I needed to figure out why I couldn't have a good relationship the way I wanted. I needed to figure out how I can find someone to lay in my bed as soon as possible. I wanted someone to get laid. I couldn't afford to let my crotch laugh at me anymore.

'See, it's very simple, girls expect more than the looks and the flashy cars you offer.'

I nodded.

Can't girls think about what boys expect? What I expect? I thought.

She continued, 'She must feel you care for her and respect her. And she should feel that you're going to stay with her, if not for lifetime then at least for quite some time to be called a relationship.'

'But…' I tried to interrupt but she cut me off and continued.

'Spend some time with her before going ahead. She should feel that you're with her because you love her and not just to pull her pants down. You need to feel for her from the bottom of your heart, not from the bottom of your zip, ONLY,' she paused and looked at me. I nodded in her support. She felt proud of herself. It showed on her face.

I wondered what to say next. I scratched my head.

'So, after doing all this I will get any girl laid?'

'Don't be so mean, Vardan. I'm talking about how you can get into a good relationship,' she shrieked. She stood up and walked towards the kitchen.

'So, physical intimacy is not the part of a good relationship? Excluding sex from a relationship makes it a good relationship?' I followed her.

She pulled out a packet of Tropicana-mixed-fruit juice from the fridge and gestured me to hold that. I did. Then she lifted three glasses and came back to the living area. I toddled behind. I waited for her to respond.

'You know what? You're really desperate,' she said, placing the glasses on table. I placed the juice packet.

'Frustrated,' interrupted Adithya.

'Hopeless,' said Sejal. She poured the juice into the glass.

'Distressed,' shouted Adithya. And they both started laughing. It hurt my ears. I stayed like a statue on the couch.

'It's not a joke. It's a serious matter,' I screamed.

'Yes, very serious, thirteen girls have refused to sleep with you, ha ha!' he said. They both high-fived each other making fun of me.

'Why don't you go and have sex with a prostitute? At least to release your frustration?' said Adithya, sipping up the juice. I felt like throwing the glass of juice on his face. But I rather controlled.

I scowled at him. I threw my hands in air, showing my disagreement.

'I will talk to Rehaan, if you say. He is a frequent visitor,' he added. Rehaan was one of our classmates.

'Are you fucking kidding me? I'm not going to give my virginity to a whore,' I screamed. As if they were just ready to drag me to a prostitute.

'Then be a potential boyfriend,' said Sejal. She puts the glass on the table and looked at me.

I nodded. 'I will try if it is so,' I mumbled.

'You must.'

'Whatever,' I shrugged my shoulders. 'I don't want to discuss this anymore. Let me rest for a while.' I kicked on Adithya's ass and covered the whole sofa and lay down as soon as he fell on the floor.

Later, we talked for a while, fought with each other and watched the latest episode of Game of Thrones.

At around 10pm, I dropped Adithya at College hostel and drove off towards home.

4.

It is bad when you have to face the person you hate the most. It is very bad when you have to face them daily. But it is even worse when the person is your father.

My mother answered the door when I reached home. And I could have sensed that my father was at home as soon as I looked at her solemn face.

'WELCOME TO THE GUEST HOUSE,' shouted my father in his faltering voice as he saw me enter. I hated this voice. It had been haunting my ears since my childhood. He clapped three times. I counted. I despised his welcome.

I turned my face to look at him. He was sitting on a chair, legs straight on dining table with a bottle of whisky, glass, ice cubes and dry fruits. *Amrut 100 Distillery Single Malt Whisky*, I read on the whisky bottle. He was in his office attire, which made me guess that he had just arrived from his office. He wore a black suite with white shirt. His black polished shoes and Rolex Watch in hand shined. He guzzled whisky almost every next day. And my mother had to spruce up his whisky table and stay awake until he slept.

'You, go to your room, I will bring you dinner there,' my mother whispered. I didn't like her to whisper unnecessarily. I glanced at her and walked to the kitchen instead. She followed me. I took out a water bottle from the fridge, gulped half of the water in one go, placed the bottle back into the fridge and started walking towards my room.

'Stop, STOP THERE. Is this the time to come home? Huh! Where were you?' suddenly, he shouted, turning his head towards me. The voice was loud enough to create an echo in the house. My left leg froze in air as I heard him. I stopped there. I squinted at him. He had hung his head down, mumbling. He sounded like a caring father. But I knew he had got an opportunity to shout. This was what he liked the most when he was home.

After not getting any response for a few seconds, he banged the table with his left hand. '*Bhenchod*! No one listens to me. I run this world, but no value at home. Nothing useful, just wasting the time,' he added, stuttering and throwing his hands in air. He stared at the whisky bottle, as if someone was inside the bottle to address his unnecessary banter. He kept the glass on table with a thumping voice as the glass was empty.

Which father abuses his son like this? I thought. Though I had to think like this daily. He used to behave badly at home without any reason. Perhaps, it made him feel like a man. A successful man, let me be more appropriate. Usually he was a rude man, but after taking few pegs of whisky he turned abusive and behaved like an animal. A hazardous animal, who fed us. He was rich and successful for rest of the world. But he failed to become a good husband as well as a good father at home.

I was about to respond but my mother held my right arm. I looked into her eyes and she looked as if she is pleading me not to utter a single word. I didn't.

'Come, come here and sit. Let's talk. I'm… I'm your father... Let me tell you what's good for you,' he said, pouring the whisky into glass. 'Why the hell are you standing there? Go and bring some ice cubes,' he added, looking at my mother. She paced towards the kitchen and came back with a bowl of ice cubes before he could fill his whisky glass.

'Didn't you hear? Come and sit here,' he shouted again. This time he gazed at me. I didn't care. Even I stared back. Then I looked at my mother. She had fixed her gaze down in fear. As if she had done something wrong. I hated my father more whenever I saw her like that. I always wondered how they had a love-marriage. Perhaps, it made me think there was nothing called *love*.

'No, I didn't. I don't and I will never hear you,' I screamed this inside my head. I wanted to scream this out. But I didn't. I walked straight to my room without responding him anything. I shut the door behind and fell on my bed. I hid my head under the pillow so that I wouldn't be able to hear him yelling. My family was not a normal family like others. Because of my father. We hardly talked with each other at home whenever he was around. My father was a peace loving man until he started shouting. So, there was always a dead silence whenever he was around. And my childhood was spent in that silence, figuring out why he was rude towards us. I didn't know how it felt when a son was hugged by his father, because my father never hugged me. According to him, pampering makes children worse. And he never pampered his only child. I didn't know how it felt when a child was praised by his father. I was never praised by my father even when I was a topper of my school. And I always wondered how was I born to such a father.

'I made it all…I had nothing when I came to Delhi. At his age…I used to struggle and work very hard. I made it all… I made it all.' I heard him shout as soon as I pulled my head out of the pillow. I had been hearing this story since my childhood. He wasn't that educated. He came to Delhi from Gorakhpur with no money, when he was very young. No doubt he worked very hard, formed his own export business, became India's one of the top exporters and earned a pile of money. But these things couldn't make him a good person, at least for me. He wanted me to join his business as soon as I completed my schooling. But I refused to do that and joined engineering instead.

Since then he turned furious towards me. That hardly affected me. Hate has no power to affect you when you don't expect love. Hate is powerless where love doesn't exist.

5.

'VARDAN...Vardannnn...' Suddenly, I heard my mother scream. It scared me. I got up quickly and rushed out of my room.

'What happened, mom?' I wailed frightened, looking around to find her. I came to living area. Then I saw my father lying on the floor near bathroom door and my mother trying to pull him up.

'You okay, mom?' I shouted, running my hands through my hair.

'Vardan, your dad fell on the floor, come and help him get up,' she boomed. She held his right arm, hand behind his neck, trying to help him get up.

'Mom, did you have your dinner?' I said instead.

'Vardan?' my mother looked at me for a while. 'Help him get up, *beta*.'

'Mom, I'm hungry...going to have my dinner. Good night,' I said and walked towards the kitchen. I scolded myself for ignoring her. I didn't feel to have anything. I just went to my room and tried to sleep.

After a few minutes, I heard my room's door open. I saw my mother enter the room.

'You're still awake, mom?' I said as she sat and placed the dinner plate on bed. She looked stressed. I sat up. I threw the quilt aside.

'How can I sleep when no one wants me to sleep peacefully? One is drowned in whisky and another in anger, all the time,' she said, angrily, and faced the other way. She pushed the plate towards me.

'Mom, are you angry with me?'

She looked at me. 'Why can't you help your own father get up?' she said, pouring the *Paneer* on rice and mixing them with a spoon. I opened my mouth wide as she gestured to feed me.

I really did not like the conversation. I wanted to gulp the whole food in plate in one go and hide under the quilt once again. But I couldn't ignore the conversation. I couldn't ignore my mother. I couldn't even swallow the food inside my mouth.

'Why can't he stop behaving rudely with his own and only son? Why can't he stop making his own wife's life worse? And even why can't he stop spreading hate in the house?' I mumbled, running my jaw, counting Paneer pieces, and circling spoon in the bowl. For that moment, my concentration on plate was as high as I could have counted the rice grains in plate. I stretched to get the water bottle from side table and gulped some water.

After a few seconds of silence, she said, 'He doesn't hate you, *beta*.'

'He doesn't love me, Mom,' I said, mouth stuffed with food.

She was speechless. She seemed hunting for words.

'This is the way he is. We cannot change someone's nature. See, he provides us everything to lead a good life. And even, he doesn't behave rudely when he is not drunk…' I cut her off before she could complete.

'Mom… Mom, he doesn't even care to talk when he is not drunk. And you know very well that he bought me that Audi because our neighbor Somanis had gifted the same Audi to their daughter Riya… in order to compete with them ,' I paused for a moment. 'Whatever. Leave this,' I said, moving backwards to signal that I was done with the dinner. I placed my head on the bed rest.

My mother shrugged her shoulders, seeing me stop eating.

'I'm done, Mom. I had something at Sejal's place. Now I want to sleep,' I said, slipping under the quilt.

'*Beta*, please never drink. I don't want you to become like your father.'

'Mom, you started again? You know I don't and I will never,' I shrieked, peeping out of the quilt. I didn't booze. I had never. Alcohol reminded me the worst part of my father. I hated it.

'Promise?'

'Promise, Mom. Now you go and sleep.'

She stood up and turned to leave.

'Please switch off the lights and have your dinner before you go to the bed. Good night.'

6.

'Where the fuck are you?' I got to hear this terrible thing as soon as I pressed the green call button, with my half open eyes. It was Adithya.

'In bed… What happened?' I murmured, yawning and pulling the quilt up to cover myself and enjoy the sleep for some more time.

'Dude, you got screwed up today. I'm in class and Avinash sir has already entered. Come fast. Bye,' he said and disconnected. I realized he was whispering. I realized my mother had tried to wake me up three times. I realized how many times I had put my phone alarm on snooze, thinking to sleep for five more minutes. I realized I had to go to the college on time that day. I realized I was late. And I realized I was a bit late to realize all these things.

My sleep just flew away. Evaporated like water. I threw out the quilt and sat up. I stared at my mobile; it was 10:06am.

'Shit man! It's too late… got screwed up… completely screwed up,' I murmured to myself.

I was in IIT Delhi and that was the first day of third semester. The first class was supposed to be taken by Prof. Avinash Rao. And he was ridiculously famous for his severity and strictness.

'He is going to beat my ass today,' I muttered, throwing my mobile on pillow beside me.

I jumped out of my bed and rushed towards the bathroom directly. Washed my face and came out quickly. Wore my denim, wrist watch, t-shirt and Nike Sneakers. I took my mobile and car's key and came out of my room, spraying the deodorant all over my body. While sprinting out of the house, I heard my mother shout my name to have the breakfast. But I was too late to have breakfast. I was too late to respond to my mother's concerns.

I threw the deodorant bottle on back seat and started the car. I drove off.

I saw Prof. Avinash and our VC inside the classroom as soon as I reached there. Immediately, I felt sweat on my forehead. I stood outside the classroom.

What the fuck is this VC doing here now? I thought.

'Good morning sir,' I greeted hesitantly as my eyes met with the VC. He looked at me. Firstly, he nodded to my greeting and then looked at his wrist watch. He shook his head and raised his right eyebrow, looking at me. He meant to tell me I was late. But a smile on his face saved me from the embarrassment. He was a cool guy unlike Prof. Avinash.

I heard a heavy voice. 'YOU ARE LATE,' shouted Prof. Avinash. As expected.

I looked at him. He was already staring at me as if expecting for an immediate answer. He looked like one of the white walkers from Game of Thrones.

I was just scratching my ass and trying to find a suitable answer, and then he shouted one more time.

'Where are your notebooks?'

I came late without notebooks and was being questioned in front of VC. I felt nervous at the moment. I looked around the classroom. Everyone was looking at me as if I was sitting on the hot seat of KBC and was at the final seven crore question and they were waiting for my answer eagerly. I didn't like that unwanted attention though.

'Sir, actually, last night I was out with my family for dinner and we came late at night. So, I couldn't sleep on time and woke up late today. I forgot to bring my notebooks as I'm coming directly from bed,' I lied. But I tried to look confident about what I said.

'So, you're coming from bed… but what about your unzipped denim?' said the VC, grinning. And suddenly, the whole class started laughing, except Prof. Avinash. I wanted to appreciate Prof. Avinash for this.

I looked down and saw my denim was unzipped. It made me feel embarrassed like hell. Seriously! I felt like I was standing naked there.

I turned to another side and zipped up my denim. I turned back and gazed at the VC with a smile on my face, mainly to save myself from self-embarrassment and pretend as if nothing happened, everything was okay.

I looked around the classroom. I saw Rohit and Mohit, two losers from my class, who sat behind my desk and were extremely unhappy with me as I got more attention than them from the girls of our class. They were giggling loudly. Having caught me glower at them, they hid under their desk. Then I looked at Divya, one of my thirteen ex-girlfriends. She was chuckling weirdly. She laughed some more in revenge as she saw me looking at her. I wanted to pull her hair out of irritation. But, I couldn't.

And then suddenly attention of the whole class diverted towards the first bench of third row as a notebook fell on the floor and a girl came out of her desk and bent down to pick that up. As she bent down, her long beautiful hair touched the ground, covering half of her face and I could see only her side face. Which I couldn't recognize. She was not from our class, in last semesters.

My mouth fell open as soon as she stood up and I saw her completely.

'OH! MY GOD,' this is what I said in my head.

She was tall. Five feet, seven inches. Slim and fair with long hair. I wanted the world to stop for a moment that I could keep looking at her narrow face with flawless skin, which might turn cream to pinkish in just one small touch. She wore a blue fitted silk suit in which her curves looked the best. She was damn beautiful. Perhaps, she was one of the most beautiful girls I had ever seen in my life.

She sat back on her seat. She was still smiling. I found that smile mischievous. And realized sometimes it's not bad to come with your unzipped jeans and get embarrassed in front of the whole class if it makes a beautiful girl smile. And then I realized I was gawking at her in presence of VC and Prof. Avinash. I turned to look at them.

'Sorry sir,' I said, looking at the VC and adjusting my jeans.

'It's okay. But next time don't forget to zip up your denim before coming to the class,' said the VC and laughed, followed by the whole class except the Prof.

'Next time, come on time,' added Prof. Avinash as I entered the class-room.

I walked to the third bench of last row and sat with Adithya.

7.

'Who is that girl, sitting with Wimp? She wasn't with us in first year,' I whispered to Adithya as soon as I sat down, nudging. Wimp was the nickname of Dimple Walia. She was kind of a studious girl who was extra nice to everyone. Four of her large teeth peeped out of her mouth all the time. Everyone in our class called her as Wimp.

'I don't want to get my ass kicked out of the class with you. So, sit silently,' he whispered back, nudging but without looking at me

'Tell me; otherwise I will kick your ass before they do it.' I declared. I was very curious to know about her that I couldn't wait for a moment.

'She is Niti... Niti Handa. She topped in last semester and changed her branch from Electronics & Communications to Computer Science. So, now she is in our class. And VC came to introduce her. Now just shut your fucking mouth,' murmured Adithya.

'She is in our class now. I will get to see her daily,' I said this to myself, giggling inside. I was very happy with her decision of changing her branch. I grinned inside happily.

'She is beautiful. No?' I said to Adithya, in a low voice.

'She is hot with her slender body, dude,' whispered Rohit from behind. I turned back and stared at him.

'Sexy! She has the best curves. Nothing in short and little unlike her name. I really liked her,' added Mohit, almost moaning. They both clapped each other's hands and started giggling. Their saliva loaded tongues were falling out of their mouth.

I wanted to thrash their faces. I said slowly with my raised eyes, 'You losers… She is out of your level. You don't deserve her. So better, just scratch your poor asses and don't even think about her. Huh!'

And the bastards lay back on the bench in a sulk, smirking weirdly. Adithya giggled.

After a few minutes, VC went out of the class and Prof. Avinash started scribbling the semester plan on board. And I started to plan that how I would talk to her.

I kept squinting at her during the class while Prof. Avinash kept talking about the different coding. She was busy in scribbling whatever Prof. said and scratched on the board. And I was busy in checking her out the best I could have. She was putting her hair behind her ear as they were falling on her face again and again. I wanted to sit beside her and hold her hair in my hand that they couldn't disturb her.

Suddenly, she stopped scribbling, put the pen between her soft pink lips and started to tie her hair behind. I wondered if she heard what I was thinking. Abruptly, I stopped looking at her and turned my face towards the Prof. But, I couldn't keep myself from squinting at her for a long. I glimpsed, her hair was in a loose bun on the top of her head now and she was back at scribbling. Her long beautiful neck was visible now. Small diamond in the center of her golden earrings twinkled as sunlight fell on it.

I wanted a girlfriend. Wanted to be in a perfect relationship, in my way. And when you desperately want someone in your life you find every next girl beautiful. But, she was actually beautiful. Something more than that!

I looked outside the window and started imagining of getting her in my arms and moving my fingers on her beautiful neck gently. I was totally lost in my thoughts that I couldn't even realize when the class got over and everyone walked out of the class.

Adithya slapped my right shoulder and brought me back to my senses.

* * *

'I really liked her. She is kind of a girl I have always desired as my girlfriend,' I said to Adithya, while toddling out of the class.

'But, you're surely not the type of a boyfriend she would ever have desired for,' said Adithya, giggling. I didn't appreciate that.

'Don't joke when I'm trying to make a serious conversation,' I uttered, moping and raising my eyes. We walked towards the parking area.

'Okay! She is beautiful, but what next?' he said, looking at his mobile.

'That I also don't know. But, I fell for her the very first time I saw her. She is fucking beautiful. Isn't she?'

'You desire for only one thing in a girl. You fell for only one thing. And you end up not getting it. Now we're going to hear your fourteenth un-suck-sex-full love story very soon?' he shouted and bent down laughingly. He was laughing alone. I wanted to kick on his ass. But I didn't. Deep down inside my heart, I got scared, thinking about the possibility of what he had just said.

'I will be careful in her case. If it works, I won't let her go. Remember, what Sejal suggested...? To become a potential boyfriend...,' I said, smirking. I unlocked my car. We sat inside.

'Well, now let me go. Drop me to Munirka,' mumbled Adithya, adjusting the seat and turning least interested in what we were talking about. He reclined himself on the comfortable seat. His girlfriend lived in a rented flat in Munirka.

'Do you guys make out every day?' suddenly, I asked him, while starting the car. I don't know what made me ask that.

He didn't respond. He looked another way instead.

After a few seconds of silence, he whispered, 'Twice a day, minimum.'

I looked at him. He was smirking. I looked another way, disappointed.

I drove off.

8.

Next day, I had reached college half an hour before the time. Had parked my car inside the college, near the entrance gate, and waited for Niti. Basically, was trying a trick to impress her by showing my sumptuous car.

I stood near my car and kept looking at the entrance. And after a few minutest, she finally appeared. I saw her entering the college. She wore blue denim and a white—and—blue striped spaghetti. She looked amazingly beautiful. Wimp was with her. Wimp's four peeping teeth walked before them.

'So, Wimp has become her friend,' I said to myself, stroking my chin. Wimp just gained some respect for herself.

I stood near the bonnet of my car, looking at them from the corner of my right eye. And then, I brought out my Ray-Ban sunglasses from the car and wore them quickly. I gently placed my left hand on the bonnet and the right hand was in jeans pocket. I pretended to look other side when I was squinting at them constantly.

There is a good thing about wearing sunglasses. You can easily stare at something while pretending to look somewhere else.

My heartbeat was increasing with every step she took to come towards me. I was expecting her to look at me and my car of course.

My heart just skipped a beat when she passed by me. I held on my car to keep myself from falling. I loved to see her going. Her tight denim re-assured the best curves she had.

As soon as I came back to life, I realized she didn't even look at me. Nor at my car. Even Wimp didn't bump into me. She always tried to find a reason to talk to me even when I always ignored her.

'May be she didn't see me,' I murmured to myself.

All the preparations went in vain. It felt bad.

I parked my car in the parking area and walked towards the classroom, while planning in my head that how I would talk to Niti.

Prof. hadn't come when I entered the classroom. I sat with Adithya. I saw Wimp giggle while talking to Niti. She was giggling alone. I abused her in my head thinking I would have talked to Niti if Wimp would have interacted with me there.

And then I bellowed, 'I got a plan.'

'What?' asked Adithya, making a puzzled face.

'Nothing,' I said without looking at him and wrote a text to Wimp without wasting time.

`Meet me outside the classroom!!!`

`When?` She wrote back. I appreciated her quick reply.

`Now! Right now!`

She sent me a confused smiley and looked at me. I gestured her to go out. And she did. She stood up and walked out of the classroom. I followed her.

'Hey, what happened? And I can't believe you asked me out,' she exclaimed, her hands on her cheeks. Her nose turned red in excitement.

I raised my eyebrows at her. 'I just asked you to come out of the classroom. And what the hell is wrong with you?' I shouted. And before she could reply I realized I had to go easy on her. She sat with Niti. I just remembered. We started toddling towards the cafeteria.

Bemused, she shrugged her shoulders.

'I mean, you just passed by me without even saying a 'hi' or anything.'

'When? I didn't notice. May be I was talking to someone?'

'I was there when you entered the college. And yes, you were with your new friend. I guess the best friend till now.'

'Oh, yes. I came with Niti. Our new classmate. We came by the same metro as she lives in Janakpuri,' she said and laughed. I couldn't understand what was funny in that. I faked a smile.

'You didn't introduce me to your new friend.' I said.

'Oh shit! How did I forget?' she shouted, slapping her head. 'I will introduce her to you now, let's go to the classroom.' I liked her overreaction though. She almost gestured to walk back to the class.

'No. Not in the classroom.' I held her hand.

'Then?'

'You will be taking her to the cafeteria in break time. I will come to you there and then you will introduce me to her. Rest I will manage.'

'Okay, I will. But, why are you so excited about her?' she asked with one eye raised.

'Because, she is the most beautiful girl in our college.'

'Am I not beautiful?' She glowered at me.

Yes, you're, when your four peeping teeth are not visible, I thought.

'Let's go to the class. Prof. would come in any second,' I said instead.

* * *

'Hey, let's go to the cafeteria. I'm feeling like having something,' shouted Wimp, looking at Niti, as soon as the break began. Her volume was loud enough to startle the rest of the students in our class. She then turned and winked at me. I tried to ignore that. They walked out of the classroom. I stayed there for next few minutes and then walked towards the cafeteria.

I saw Wimp and Niti sitting in an alcove in one corner of the cafeteria when I reached there. Wimp was pushing the Sandwich in her mouth and Niti was pulling up lemonade with a straw.

'You can have it slowly like a normal human, no one is taking it away from you,' I said and smirked, pulling up a chair.

'Hey, actually, I was hungry, so…,'said Wimp and laughed. She covered her mouth with right hand so that Sandwich in her mouth wouldn't fall out.

I sat there with confidence as if they were waiting for me. 'Yes, looks like,' I said.

'Niti, that's Vardan. He is also in our class,' said Wimp, looking at Niti. She went back to mince her Sandwich. I and Niti looked at each other. That was my first eye contact with her. I looked into her eyes. There was something special in her eyes that I didn't want to stop looking at them. But I had to. I offered my hand to her. We shook hands.

'Yes, I saw him the very first day. He came late that day,' said Niti, smirking.

'That too with unzipped denim,' added Wimp and started laughing. Niti joined her. They both laughed together and I smiled to save myself from the unexpected embarrassment.

Fuck you, Wimp.

'I woke up late that day and couldn't care about anything but reaching college as soon as possible. Anyways, nice name, Niti, short and sophisticated.' I ended trying to change the topic.

'Thanks, you too have a good name,' said Niti, trying to hide her smile behind her palm.

'It's Vardan Awasthi. My full name,' I said, gazing at her.

'Mine is Niti Handa. Full name, you know,' she smirked sarcastically.

'I really liked this surname. Handa… unique one.'

'Awasthi is also not bad,' she said and laughed. I and Wimp joined.

I ordered a mince for myself. 'So, you changed your branch?' I asked her.

But, Wimp shouted before Niti could reply, 'Hey, he will help you in coding. He is very good at that.' I wanted to buy Wimp few more Sandwiches for saying that.

'Yes, just let me know if you need any help, as you're new to our branch,' I said.

'Sure,' she said. She took a big sip of lemonade.

We talked for a little, while Wimp attacked on two more Sandwiches. I finished my mince.

'You had to leave early today, no? Vardan will drop you,' shouted Wimp, suddenly, looking at Niti. Then she looked at me and winked. I looked another way to hide the excitement and happiness on my face. I really wanted to pat Wimp's shoulder for what she had just said. I had never expected such intelligence from her.

'No, it's okay, I will manage,' said Niti.

'It's completely okay. I will drop you. Even I have some work in Janakpuri,' I said and abruptly my tongue fell out of my mouth as soon as I realized I mentioned the place name she lived in.

'How do you know I live in Janakpuri? I guess I haven't told you yet?' she asked, moving her suspicious eyes up and down. I didn't know what to say next. I squeezed my knees under the table.

And then, Wimp started clapping, 'What a guess, Vardan. You have always been good at guessing.' Her overacting reflected in those loud claps. She winked twice looking at me.

'Actually, ummm…I just mentioned Janakpuri, because I have some work there. You live in Janakpuri? That's nice,' I said smiling and looked other way.

She shook her head.

'So, we will leave the class after next lecture. Okay?'

'Okay, fine,' said Niti. I giggled inside.

You're too nice, Wimp.

Break got over and we walked towards the class. Rohit and Mohit hit their heads on bench seeing me enter with Niti.

9.

Niti stood up and left the class as soon as the next lecture was winded up. I followed her.

'Where do you live in Janakpuri?' I said while unlocking my car. We sat inside.

'C-block, near Channan Devi Hospital,' she said, putting her bag on her lap. She adjusted herself in the seat. She didn't look much like a talker—according to my prejudgment.

'You know that place?' she added, breaking the silence there. I wondered if she sensed my prejudgment about her.

'Yes. Yes, I do…,' I paused looking at her. 'Well, can we have a coffee together? There is a coffee shop on the way. They make the best coffee in the city,' I said, hesitantly. I don't know why, but this was the first time when I felt less of courage to ask a girl for coffee, that too sitting in my car—where I felt super confident.

I wondered if she denies and runs out of the car. Feeling of disappointment started growing in my blood as she didn't say anything for next few seconds. She just stared at her wrist watch.

'Hope, it's not too much for you,' I shrugged.

'No, not like that. I'm just thinking if I will get late...,' she paused. And my heart too went on a pause mode, till the moment she continued. 'Okay, let's have one...but we can't sit there for a long time as I'm already getting late.'

There is a time when you're happy and can smile to express it. And, there comes a time when you're extremely happy, but can't even express it. And that was my time. I just giggled inside.

'Sure,' I said and drove off. And in next few minutes, we were sitting in a nearby cafe. We ordered cold coffee, because she liked that.

I kept twirling the straw in coffee mug, figuring out what to say next, how to start a conversation.

'Came to know that you topped in last semester, yet changed your branch?' I asked when I hardly cared about her branch and all. My eyes were all on her, amazed seeing her too near.

She dabbed the napkin on her lips as a small drop of coffee fell on her lower lips. 'I always wanted to do engineering in computer science, but couldn't make it at the time of admission. So, changed my branch to CS when got an opportunity.'

'How strange,' I mumbled, looking into her eyes.

'Strange?' she shrugged her shoulders.

'I mean how strange that despite being in the same college, we never saw or met each other.'

She smiled.

'Yes, even I can't recall seeing you. Maybe because, I studied most of the time and left for home as soon as the class got over.'

'Like you're going to leave today,' I said. We both laughed. You feel a sense of comfort as soon as you realize that the girl has started laughing during your first conversation. I reclined in my chair.

'Dimple told me that you're really good at coding,' she said, while checking her mobile. I felt to ask for her number, but then I dropped the idea thinking it was too early to ask for number.

'Yes, I like coding. I will help you in that as you're new to CS. And you can call Dimple as Wimp, her nick name in the college,' I smirked. I had lied about liking coding. Otherwise, coding sucked more than engineering.

She grinned. 'Why do you call her as Wimp?'

I told her the little story of how that Wimp name was created. She laughed about that. I wanted to repeat so that she could laugh one more time. But I didn't. She offered to pay the half bill. I resisted. Though, none of the girls I dated had allowed me to have sex with them. But also, none of them had ever offered to pay the half bill. Money hardly mattered to me, but the gesture did. It felt like a signal to me that she wasn't the type of a girl, who was going to get impressed by me like other girls. Niti insisted to pay her part. I didn't let her pay but settled promising her that she would pay when we would have our next coffee together.

We talked some more before coming out of that cafe. I learnt a little about her. She stayed alone in Janakpuri as her family was in Hisar, Haryana. Her schooling was from Springdales School, Dhaula Kuan. Between our short conversations, I wanted to tell her how beautiful she looked, specially while smiling. Wanted to kiss her on her pink lips when she looked right into my eyes. And wanted to ask her if she was single. But, sincere-me didn't allow me to do anything like that.

We sat in my car and headed towards Janakpuri. There was traffic on our way and that was the first time I was loving it.

'So, you have been living alone since schooling?'

'No, I lived at my uncle's place in Saket. After schooling I shifted to Janakpuri.'

You did a great job of shifting there alone, I thought, giggling inside. A part of me imagined myself in her apartment where she lived alone.

We talked about our course and college, laughed and smiled a few times during our ride to Janakpuri. I stopped the car as we reached her flat.

'See you tomorrow in college,' I said.

'Sure. And you told that you had some work in Janakpuri?' she mumbled while getting out of the car. She held on the car door, waiting for me to respond.

'Yes, I had to drop someone,' I said, grinning. She blushed and pushed the door shut. She turned away to leave.

* * *

'Fuck beautiful. I heard this hundreds of times during our ten minute conversation,' screamed Sejal. That day, after dropping Niti, I directly went to Sejal's place. I told her about Niti—from seeing her first time in class till I had dropped her few hours back. Sejal was busy in making her college project and I was trying to make her listen to my new girl's story. And I was so excited about Niti that I couldn't forget to mention how beautiful she was after every sentence I told to Sejal.

'But she is beautiful. Why would you feel jealous of her,' I blurted out, giggling.

'Then go and fuck with her. Let me focus on my project work,' she shouted, pulling a rolled chart paper from table. She sat on the wooden floor, put her right foot on one corner of the chart, bent forward and spread that with her hands. As if explaining me how I could have fucked Niti on the floor.

'Only, if she allows me, I won't mind,' I said, and laughed weirdly.

'Jerk,' she shouted. She went ahead drawing some lines on the chart. I went to kitchen to bring a water bottle from the fridge. I gulped some water.

She stood up. 'What happened after that?' she said, snatching the water bottle from my hand.

'I have just come to you after dropping her. I wanted to ask for her number. But I didn't. I wanted to ask if she has a boyfriend. But I didn't. I wanted to ask her if she would help me to get rid of the baggage of being a virgin. But I didn't,' I stopped to grin. 'I thought I would do this in my next date with her,' I ended, falling up on the sofa. I picked up the remote lying on table and switched on the television.

'Date? Hmmm…' she paused to chuckle. 'It's good to go slow and create a good bond before going ahead. Otherwise, your virgin misery will follow some more,' she paused one more time realizing that the television was on now. 'Vardan, don't start this bullshit. I won't be able to focus on my project otherwise. It's really urgent,' she protested, her hands moving in air.

'Fuck your project till the time I'm here,' I shouted and stretched my legs in the comfortable sofa. I kept one more cushion beneath my head and felt more relaxed. 'And don't worry. I'm keeping that Potential Boyfriend thing in my mind this time. Let's see if this works.'

'Good to become a potential boyfriend than a desperate fucker,' she said. She sat on the couch. 'And, I will do this project work after you leave. But, I need the remote now.' She crawled toward sofa and attacked the remote. I caught that with my full strength and defended. But after a few seconds of scuffle, she succeeded to snatch the remote from my hand.

10.

Every break up breaks you to the core, turning you into a pessimist and pushing you to feel like the world is not a good place for you. Nothing is left for you. And then a beautiful girl walks in and turns you into more optimist than you ever were. You suddenly realize that the world is still beautiful. A lot to explore.

I knocked on the door. I was standing outside Niti's apartment, holding the thick fat engineering books in my hand. It'd been more than a week since my first coffee with Niti. And it was very unusual for me to be with a girl without flirting this long. But I did. Anyways, we talked daily after that day. We talked in classroom, sat in college cafeteria and grew some friendship between us. And yesterday, we—I, Niti, Wimp and Adithya had gone for a movie and after movie I and Niti decided that I'd come to her place in the morning, help her in study to cover her first and second semester syllabus and then we would go to the college together. I was very excited about that.

I pressed the bell button for the third time. And then finally, the door got half open.

My lungs denied taking oxygen for a few seconds when my eyes recognized her. My eyeballs were about to jump out. She had held on the half open door. She was in pink night shorts and white tee. Her shorts barely covered her half thighs. She was looking voluptuously hot.

'Hi,' she mumbled, rubbing her right eye and bringing me back to life. My mouth was wide open, words still denied to come out.

I smiled. She opened the door to signal me in.

'You came too early. I just woke up,' she blurted out, yawning. I stepped inside her apartment. I looked around. It was a nice two-bed-room-furnished flat, with a spacious living room. I stared at the watch dangled on wall in front of me and realized it was just 7am. I kept the books on table.

'Oh, really? I didn't realize that I woke up too early today,' I said. I hadn't even slept last night. She shut the door. She removed books and other stuffs from sofa and gestured me to sit there. She made herself comfortable on the opposite sofa. She was still in her sleep. She rested her head on sofa-rest.

Beautiful girl like you deserves lazing around, I thought. She had closed her eyes. She looked innocent like hell. An innocent who looked extremely hot though. I was looking at her face instantly and smiling.

She got up and tried to sit straight, twisting her body. Her hair fell on her face.

'Hey! Sorry. Actually, I slept late last night… so,' she murmured.

'No, it's okay. You can have a short sleep if you want,' I said, smiling. I was being more gentle than I could ever imagine of myself. And then my eyes fell on her long and beautifully carved bare legs, as if made of white marbles. Most beautiful pair of legs I had ever seen in my life. I stared at them for a few seconds and then looked other way. She could catch me and consider me as desperate. Maybe I was desperate, but I didn't want her to know that.

'Finally, I'm out of my sleep,' she grinned, 'I thought you wouldn't come,' she said, tying her hair behind. Her eyes still half open.

Are you even serious? How could I miss the opportunity? How could I not come?

I shrugged my shoulders.

'Remembering about the first class, I didn't think you could wake up this early,' she said and started laughing. I joined her. I laughed and squinted at her legs. I genuinely wanted to touch them.

'I could have come earlier if I knew you look more beautiful in the morning,' I smirked. She stopped laughing. I wondered if she didn't like my surprise compliment. I immediately dropped the idea of complimenting her beautiful bare legs.

'Beautiful? In this messy hair? Huh!' she ran her right hand in her hair. 'Well, Thank you,' she added before I could reply. She smiled. I smiled back. She stood up.

'Give me ten minutes. Need to get freshen up and take a shower,' she said. I nodded. I wanted to ask her if I could join her in shower. But I didn't.

11.

She was in a white-and-blue *salwar-kameez* when she came out of the bathroom after eighteen minutes. I had counted every single minute. She still looked beautiful, but I had lost half of my view now. Damn!

She came and sat on opposite sofa, dabbing her hair with the towel in her hand. Girls look more gorgeous with drenched hair, my observation though.

'I don't think you would have had your breakfast? So, what would you like to have?' she said, throwing the towel away.

You, I thought. By the way, I was seriously hungry. Even for the food.

'Anything, you offer,' I said, smiling.

'Unfortunately, my maid is on leave today. So, can't offer tea or coffee as she brings the milk,' she said. 'Let's bake some bread and prepare omelet. Hope you're not a guest here,' she added, chuckling. I shook my head. Of course I wasn't a guest there. I wanted to be a frequent visitor now.

She stood up and walked towards her kitchen. I followed her. She took out brown bread and butter from the fridge. She gestured me to hold them when I wanted to hold her. Then she took out four eggs from the fridge.

'Nice kitchen. Even nice apartment,' I said. I kept bread and butter on the kitchen rack.

'Thank you! Well, I'm preparing omelet. You, please place butter on the bread till then.'

I nodded, even when I had never done that in my whole life. I didn't know if placing butter on bread was a part of becoming a potential boyfriend. I somehow did. She prepared the omelet, baked those diligently buttered breads and we came out of the kitchen. She walked towards her bedroom. I followed her. We sat on her bed.

'You live here alone?' I asked as I lifted a bread slice.

'Yes. For last one year now.'

'It's a big flat. How much rent do you pay for it?' I said and suddenly realized how poor I was talking. Which guy asks a girl—being alone in her apartment and sitting with her in bed—that how much rent she pays? I scared if this going slow thing could turn me into a loser and tarnish my finesse in dealing with girls.

She laughed. I wondered if she heard what I was thinking. I wasn't sure why she was laughing but I joined her in the laughter anyway.

'I don't have to pay any rent, because this place is registered on my mother's name,' she said, smirking.

'Oh! So, your mother lives with your family in Hisar?'

'She isn't alive,' said Niti. And my hands froze in air as soon as I heard that, a piece of omelet still in my right frozen hand. You can't keep eating when someone mentions that their mother is dead. Even you cannot breathe for a moment. I was just shocked and felt chocked for a moment.

'I'm sorry… I didn't…' I almost fumbled. I hunted for words. I didn't know how and what to react on that. I looked at her. She was looking another way.

'It's okay. I lost her when I was seven. It hardly matters now,' she said. She went back on eating.

I wanted to ask her that how did she lose her mother, but couldn't gather courage. I sat there clueless.

After a few minutes of awkward silence, I asked, 'Who all are there in your family?'

'Father, an elder brother, grandfather, uncles, aunties and cousins. A joint family you know.'

'What do they do?'

'My father is a local politician and my brother is just trying to be like him. He somehow completed his graduation last year. I came to know,' she said, taking the last piece of bread in her mouth. She stood up and walked toward the kitchen.

'You came to know?' I asked following her to the kitchen. She put the plates inside the sink.

'Yes. My cousin who lives in Delhi told me.' She turned the tap on and washed her hands. She moved a bit and gestured me to wash my hands. I did.

'So, you don't talk to your…' she cut me off before I could complete.

'What about you? Who all are there in your family?' she asked. We came and sat on the sofa in living room.

'Just Mom, Dad and I. My father has an export business and mother is a homemaker.'

'Nice,' she said. She joined me on the sofa I was sitting. She sat beside me. She picked a book from the table.

'Thanks for bringing these books,' she said, looking at me. I nodded, smiling. I was wondering to say something, basically to distract my attention from her lips which were very near to mine. It was very tough to concentrate on books while sitting with her.

'By the way, why are you always in hurry to leave right after the class ends?'

'So that I can spend some time with my kids?' she said, smiling. I didn't appreciate that smile. She smiled alone.

Kids? What the fuck she is talking about? I thought.

I shrugged my shoulders, lifting my eyebrows up and making my face startled. 'Kids?'

She started laughing louder. I didn't join her in laughter until she broke the suspense.

'I go to an NGO and teach some unprivileged children there. You know, I love children,' she said in between the laughter. I took a sigh of relief.

'You love children and I love the process how they are born,' I murmured to myself.

'That's really a great thing,' I said and joined her in laughter. She lifted a book from the table and we started studying now. And for next half an hour, we talked about studies only.

'Do you have a boyfriend?' I asked suddenly. And this sudden out of syllabus question had startled her a bit. That could be seen on her face.

'Suddenly?'

'Just wanted to know,' I smirked.

'I haven't been in any such relationships yet.'

'So, you're single since birth?' I smirked. I shut my mouth and thought, *what a lame joke, Vardan*.

'Technically, yes,' she laughed louder.

'How can this beautiful girl be single?'

'Study and the NGO thing couldn't let her think about this,' she winked, smiling, 'Thanks for the compliment by the way.'

'Nice.'

'Nice?'

'I mean, nice. You're focused in your studies,' I blurted out. I was extremely happy about her being single.

'Do you have a girlfriend?' she asked. And I went on a pause mode. *How come I didn't expect this question? How?* I wondered what to respond. I wondered how she would react if I tell her about my thirteen un-suck-sex-full—that's how my friends pronounce it, relationships.

'I'm SINGLE,' I said, emphasizing the last word, 'But, I have been in a few relationships, none of them lasted for a long,' I grinned. I didn't know why but I was feeling like a culprit.

She nodded, going back to the book in her hand. She started studying again. For next few minutes, we studied and then left for the college.

12.

Three weeks later

It's damn borin! Let's go out smwhr, she wrote me a text between the lectures.

Where? I wrote back.

Anywhere, bt can't sit here anymore, she texted.

I looked at her. She wore a painful and boring expression on her face. She walked out of the classroom as I sent her a thumps up emoji. I said Adithya bye and left the class.

I and Niti had grown a very good bond by then. Sejal and Adithya appreciated and motivated me for that. We talked most of the time in college, sometimes we sat together in class. We used to chat daily through text messages, missed lectures, and visited places together, also shared bills—even when I resisted the best I could. I kept going to her place often in the morning and we studied there. Deep inside my heart, I was enjoying this. That was very new for me to hang out and spend a good amount of time with any girl without even touching her with lust.

Anyway, what I could know about Niti in last few weeks was—except the fact that she was extremely beautiful. She was the one who doesn't speak much, but when she does—you would love to listen to her. She was serious about her studies, but that couldn't stop her from being a fun loving person. Her eyes gleamed with delight and an imp smile always glittered on her face. She had a class, she wore good dresses and accessories, but she wasn't one of those girls who always talked about their dresses, parties and flings. She was a good human being, she really cared about people around, she loved children, and went to an NGO regularly. She was completely poles apart than the girls I had been with before her. Every moment I spent with her, I felt like, *SOMETHING IS DIFERENT ABOUT THIS GIRL. SOMETHING IS DIFERENT ABOUT THIS GIRL.* I desperately wanted to have a relationship with her—in my way of course. But more than that, I wanted her in my life now. And yes, she too had started enjoying my company. Everyone in college gossiped that we were dating each other. But for Niti, I was a close friend—yet. And for me and my friends, I was on a right track to become a potential boyfriend.

'Sometimes these lectures suck,' she said as I reached close to her stomping. She tied her hair behind. I could feel the deodorant she had used. It smelt good.

'They always do,' I said and laughed. She joined in my laughter.

'Well, where to go?' I asked, gesturing to walk towards the parking area.

'Wait, Vardan! We're not going in the car. Let's walk outside the college and then figure out where to go.'

'But, it's very hot. The scorching sun outside will suck us whole,' I made a face, covering my eyes with right hand as if the whole sun had come over my head.

'It will be fun. We will just walk or take an Auto.'

'Is she serious? She prefers Auto over an Audi?' I murmured to myself.

I couldn't resist as she held my arm and started dragging me. We walked towards the main gate. I felt few water drops falling on my face as soon as we stepped outside the college. I realized it was drizzling.

'Shit! Seems it is raining,' I shouted, looking up.

'It's just drizzling. It came to save you from the brutal sun,' she chuckled, 'Let's keep walking. Few water drops won't drench us,' she said, her head up towards the sky, feeling water droplets on her face.

'I think we should go back and get into the car,' I said, taking few steps back. I hid myself near the security room at college entrance. She insisted to walk under the drizzle, but I denied. I seriously didn't like the idea of getting drenched and walking in mud all around. I asked her to stay there until I come back with my car. And I ran towards the parking area. I ran as fast as I could.

* * *

I looked around, but she wasn't there. I drove the car outside college and recognized her standing at one side of the road. She was allowing rain drops to hit on her face, her head up and hands on cheeks as if standing under the shower. It had started raining.

I pressed the left door glass button down and shouted for her name, 'Hey, Niti.'

She looked at me and smiled. She gestured me with her hands to join her. I shook my head. She came near and peeped inside the car through window.

'Hey, come out. Let's have some rain-fun,' she said, grinning. Her face seemed dripping wet. Few water drops rested on her eyelashes, but a small drop of water oozed down her face and disappeared touching her soft pink lips.

'See, it can start raining heavily. You can get all drenched. Come and sit inside.'

'I'm going to enjoy this rain today. You can join me. Trust me you will also enjoy that.'

'I will enjoy seeing you in this case,' I smiled. She moved ahead and started enjoying that rain. I turned the wiper on so that I could see her clearly through front windshield. She sat on the car bonnet, spread her arms and looked up towards the sky. I could feel water drops hitting on her face. She stood up, freed her hair, toddled few steps ahead and twirled around as if making a circle. She was almost dancing like a ten-year-old. That brought an unintentional smile on my face. Then I looked at the delighted smile on her face. She looked the happiest person on this earth. I was wondering how one can be this much happier because of mere rainfall. I almost forgot to blink for a moment. I was constantly staring at her, smiling. She looked more beautiful. And suddenly, as if something magical happened to me, I parked my car aside near the college gate, got out of it and strode across the road towards her.

'You came,' she exclaimed.

'Yes, I did,' I mumbled, running my right hand through my hair, and looking into her beautiful eyes. Then I looked down. She was drenched. She wore a white tee and black denim. Her wet-almost-transparent-upper clothes had clung to her body and I could see what she was wearing inside. I tried hard not to stare at them but I couldn't. That was the first time I gaped more than her pretty face and bare legs. I squinted at her black inner and half peeping breasts, wanting badly to help them come out. She was voluptuous! Then my eyes slid down at her slim, glimmering stomach, water droplets gathered all around. She was partially naked. Almost. It aroused me badly. She was just few inches away from me, almost half bare and looking prettier in her drenched hair. I wanted to put my arms around her waist and pull her close, as close as I could feel her breathe. Wanted to put my lips on hers and plonk her on my car bonnet kissing. I wanted whole world to stop for a moment that I could keep looking at her.

'Hey, what happened?' she shook me. Startled, I regained my senses.

'Ummm…no, nothing. Rain… I didn't know walking under rain could be this much fun. Thanks!' I muttered, smirking. I put my hands in my jeans pocket.

'See, I told you,' she smiled. She held my left hand and said pulling me, 'Let's walk.'

And just after three and half seconds, she left my hand. *I won't mind if you keep holding my hand*, I thought. Well, we started walking through the black wet road. Meanwhile, while walking, her hand touched mine a few times. Strangely, this was completely a new experience for me. I could never imagine that even just a touch could feel that better. I didn't know if it felt better than sex, but it was amazing.

'Where are we going?' I asked.

'Let's have tea, rain and a hot cup of tea—world's best combination,' she exclaimed, almost jumping. It was still drizzling.

'Tea…? Okay, let's go back to the car. We will go to any café,' I said, gesturing to turn back.

'No, Vardan. We will stop at any tea-stall. Let's keep walking.'

'TEASTALL? TEASTALL? TEASTALL…?' startled me, murmured to myself. I had never tasted tea at any tea-stalls in my entire life. Even when my friends Sejal and Adithya insisted me, I always denied. You can call me an asshole, but I hated poor people and doing poor things. That reminded me of my drunken-father. I wondered how to deny her.

'See, Niti…ummm… I know a good café nearby. They serve the best tea.'

'You know nothing, Vardan. You don't know anything about the rain. Nor about the right moment,' she mumbled, smiling. That smile hit me deep. I tried to smile back, but failed as my upper lip rose a bit and fell down to shut my mouth back. I didn't say anything. Just started walking behind her.

13.

We stopped at a tea-stall, to experience something new with her—completely different than what I was longing for. It had stopped raining now. But we could still feel few fine water drops falling on us, enough to keep us wet. She sat on a busted wooden table there. I sat next to her, reluctantly. She ordered two cups of tea.

'Are you okay?' she asked, sensing an awkward silence there.

'Yes, of course. I'm enjoying it,' I faked a smile.

'Then what's with the withered face?'

'Honestly, this walking under the rain and sitting on a conked out wooden table at a tea-stall is something very new to me. But I'm really enjoying it. I do,' I smirked, 'but, still not sure about the tea,' I added, chuckling. She chuckled back.

'So, you're going to miss me next time you take shower under a rain or have tea at any tea-stall,' she winked, simpering. *Oh God*! That wink with a smile on her face pierced into my heart.

'I never want to forget about you now,' I murmured to myself.

'Yes, of course, a good company is always missed,' I winked back. And then, the large sized, fat and round faced tea seller turned to us to serve the tea. He gave both of us a disposable cup and started pouring tea from tea-kettle in his hand. I noticed he was staring at Niti while pouring the tea into our cups. I wanted to smash his face. He looked other way sensing me glare at him. He poured the tea and went back to his place, squinting at me.

Niti put the cup on table, 'It's very hot' she made a shrill voice.

'Oh, what a coincidence. Mine too,' I laughed at my own lame joke, placing my cup on the table next to hers. She chortled and stood up.

'What happened?'

'Nothing. Going to take two extra cups.'

'Oh, you sit, I will do that,' I said, getting up. I couldn't let her go to that nastily gawking tea seller. So, I went to him and fetched two empty cups. We sat back on the table. She poured half of her tea in one of those empty cups. I followed her and did the same. Then she whiffed. And I followed her again. She chuckled seeing me doing that. I wanted to keep on whiffing if that made her chuckle.

She sipped her tea. I wanted to stop following her now. But I couldn't. Grudgingly, I took my first sip. And surprisingly, it tasted nice. Much better than what I had expected. Took few more sips and remembered what she had said few minutes back *rain and tea, world's best combination.*

'So?'

'It tastes nice. Even better,' I took a big sip.

She smiled.

'You always do this?'

'This?' Her right eyebrow raised up enough from one side to make a question mark.

'This rain and tea thing,' I said. She laughed to herself. I felt like an effortless funny person.

'I don't drench myself every time it rains,' she stopped to laugh and took her last sip. 'But, yes, I can't resist myself when I'm at NGO with children and it rains.'

Fuck! Is she considering me one of those homeless, underprivileged, poor kids? I thought. I smiled weirdly and took the last sip. That last sip didn't taste as better as the first sip did.

'So, what's up with the NGO thing? How is it going?'

'It always feels amazing to be with the kids,' she exclaimed, 'And you know, four new kids have come…' suddenly she stopped and started looking the other way. I turned to follow her gaze. She had fixed her eyes on a little boy waddle towards us, carrying a plastic bag on his back with right hand and holding his pants with left. He looked like a ten-year-old. I saw he stood beside the tea-stall and bend himself forward to unload that bag on his back. He fell on the ground while dropping it down. It seemed really heavy. He immediately got up and pushed the bag under stall. And then his pants got slipped down. He wasn't wearing underwear. He immediately pulled his pants up. It made me chuckle. I looked at Niti, she had an intense look on her face. She called for that little boy. He toddled towards us and stood near silently. I looked at him up and down. He had small and dry hair. He wore a dirty vest and black unzipped pants. I counted, there were total—big and small—seven holes in his vest and some peeping threads from the holes signified that once the vest was white. His left hand was still on his pants, to keep that in place. I noticed there was a rope around his pants, in place of belt. It seemed he had not taken shower for months. I realized he was stinking. I covered my nose with right hand, but immediately removed it from there finding Niti stare at me.

14.

'What's your name?' asked Niti. The little kid looked down, moving his body incessantly and digging the ground with his right toe, as if his name was written under the ground. She repeated her question, politely.

'Shyam,' mumbled the kid, still looking down and moving his head.

'What are you doing here? Is he your father?' asked Niti.

'I work here,' he stopped for a few seconds and then continued, 'my father works at a building construction site and mother cooks foods at home.' He pointed his finger towards the right. It was really innocent of him to give that extra information.

'How much money do you get here?'

'I don't know. My father gets the money,' he made his first eye contact with us. 'But I get tea and snacks here daily,' he giggled. I noticed his yellow teeth and two front teeth missing.

'What were you carrying in that bag?' I interrupted. I too wanted to be a part of that interrogation.

He started counting on his fingers.

'Eight kg milk,' he showed eight of his fingers and then folded his fingers back to his palms. 'Three kg sugar and one kg tea,' he unfolded two of his right hand fingers and showed one finger from left hand. Suddenly my view of looking at him got changed. I loved the innocence on his face.

'Don't you go to school?' asked Niti.

'What are you doing there? Pick those empty cups and pour the milk in container,' suddenly, the tea seller screeched.

'I used to go. I went till third standard,' said the little boy and ran away chuckling.

Niti stood up and gestured towards that tea seller. I removed my purse from back pocket, thinking she was going to pay.

'Don't you think it's wrong to get a little kid work here? He should be going to school now,' said Niti politely to that tea-seller.

'Madam, what's your problem? Why do you care when his family doesn't have any issues? Do your work and let me do mine,' shouted that tea seller and went back on pouring the tea in kettle.

I put the money on his stall and held Niti's hand, 'Let's go.'

She removed her hand from mine. I saw she was fuming. I saw the kid hid under the stall. He peeped out with his one eye.

'This is the problem no one cares. Do you even know this is a crime to have a little child work here? You should release this child and never get any children to work here. Imagine if he is your child,' screamed Niti. I couldn't get what was going on. I scratched my head.

That tea-seller started laughing weirdly. Two more men sitting there, sipping the hot tea, started laughing and chuckling with him.

'These kids don't deserve to go to school. His fate is written here. And what crime? I give money to his father. You go. Don't waste your time,' said the tea-seller between his weird laughter. That infuriated Niti more.

'There is no use of talking to you? I should call the police and they will talk to you, huh,' muttered Niti. I wanted to interrupt, but didn't know what to say.

'I am not scared of anyone. Do whatever you want to do, just get away from my stall,' shouted the tea-seller almost coming near to Niti.

I don't know what happened to me suddenly, I pushed that tea-seller very hard and shouted loudly, 'Be in your limits… and stay away from her… you *motherfucker*.'

Niti held me on my left arm. And I realized I was going to smash that bastard if she hadn't pulled me back. She was still holding my hand. I felt good about that. I saw her dialing hundred-number.

'Are you seriously calling the cops?' I asked looking at Niti.

'Yes. This *moron* must learn a lesson. Didn't you see how shameless he is? Also, I can't leave that little kid like this.'

I nodded.

She finally called the cops. And I kept pulling my hair, scratching my scalp and biting my nails until the cops came. Two aged cops in a police van came there.

'Who dialed the hundred-number?' one of the cops said looking at us.

'I did,' said Niti. The cop shook his head.

'What happened?' asked the cop. She told him everything and demanded an immediate rescue for that little boy.

After few seconds of ponder, that cop said, 'You go, we will take care of it.' They gestured to move.

'But you haven't said anything to that tea seller yet,' shouted Niti.

'Madam, don't you understand? We know our job. You go home now, we will take care of this,' shouted the second cop. They turned and started walking towards the van.

'No. I won't go anywhere until you do something about it,' declared Niti loudly, folding her hands furiously. I too folded my hands in her support.

Both the cops looked at each other. They whispered something to each other for next few minutes and had a word with that tea-seller before walking to us.

'You both sit in the van,' said one of the cops.

'Why? Why should we sit there?' I asked.

'To go to the police station with us, some formalities needs to be done,' said the second cop.

Police station? No, I won't go? I will never go to that creepy place, I thought.

'What formalities?' asked Niti.

'You will know that there,' said the cop. I wanted to run away from there. But I didn't.

'Hey! We should go now. We have done our part. I don't think going to the police station would be a good idea,' I whispered to Niti.

'No, I will go to the police station if it takes to get that little boy released from here,' she shouted and my tongue fell out of my mouth. I nodded, rubbing my right hand on neck.

She moved towards the police van. I followed her as I couldn't leave her alone in that situation. I looked at that tea seller, he was smiling weirdly.

'Sit there,' said one of those cops, pointing at a bench there. We were brought to a nearby police station. It was a hell of new experience day for me. We sat on that steel bench. The cops who had brought us there walked away. And for next fifteen minutes, we kept sitting on that uncomfortable steel bench, wondering what was going on there. And then a middle aged police man walked towards us. While walking towards us, he shamelessly scratched his balls, and made face expressions as if enjoying the itching-orgasm. He sat on a chair beside our bench. We slid in our bench, making a distance from him.

'What's your name?' said that cop. *ASI Nitish Rathi*, I read on his batch.

'I'm Vardan and she is my friend Niti,' I said, looking at that cop. He wrote that on a pad in his hand.

'Friend or…?' murmured that cop, smiling weirdly. We didn't answer to that. We glared at him instead. He looked another way finding us glare at him.

'What were you both doing there?' mumbled the cop, not looking at us, facing down.

'*WHAT WERE WE DOING THERE*? What kind of a question is this? What's going on here,' yelled Niti, standing up. I too stood up and held her hand, trying to stop her.

'Don't shout here. This is a police station, not your home,' the cop yelled back.

'Then what should I do now? Your cops didn't say anything to that tea-seller, didn't do anything about that little kid and brought us here instead. We have been sitting here clueless for last half an hour before you came. And now you're asking irrelevant questions, scratching your balls. Tell me, what we're supposed to do now? Tell me?' screamed Niti. Her voice echoed in the whole police station. Everyone looked at us.

The cop glared at us fuming. 'I don't know what you're talking about, you have been brought here because you scuffled with that tea-seller, beat him, abused him, threatened him and disturbed the public peace…' blurted out that cop, 'And now I will also frame the charge of misbehaving with a police personnel. You seem drunk. Call your parents,' he said and walked away before we could respond.

15.

'WHAT THE FUCK? What the fuck is going on here? What is he talking about? We're in a police station or somewhere else?' said Niti, heaving her hands in air, disappointed. She looked extremely tired. I made her sit on the bench. Now I had to take us out of that creepy place. I couldn't let that happen anymore now. With a heavy heart, I decided to call my father. My father's just one call could make all those cops pee in their pants. But I stopped, thinking he would curse me for years after a few pegs of whisky if he came to know that I was taken to a police station. I thought not to call him, but then I looked at Niti's wilted face. And I immediately decided to call my dad.

I was just about to dial my father's number, and then Niti came to me. 'Hey, don't worry, I'm calling someone and we will be out of here very soon,' she said and walked away.

'Are you sure?' I shouted behind.

She turned back and nodded. I pushed my mobile into my jeans pocket. I sat on the bench while she talked on her mobile.

After, around, twenty minutes, I saw a tall girl, having huge ass, enter the police station. She walked towards us. As Niti recognized her she ran and fell into that tall girl's arms. Niti started sobbing. I felt bad for her.

'It's okay baby. Everything is going to be fine. We're here now,' consoled that tall girl and put her arms around Niti. They hugged tightly. I wanted to join them.

'Where is Samar?' asked Niti, coming out of that tall girl's arms and running her fingers near her left eye to remove a tear drop from there.

'He is parking the car,' mumbled the tall girl. Niti nodded. I wondered who they were talking about.

And then, a guy in red t-shirt wearing sunglasses came there. He was tall with sixteen inches biceps and broad chest. He looked like a gym freak—a bag of steroids. And then I saw Niti ran to him and they hugged. They hugged very tight. Niti almost got buried inside his chest. She sobbed some more. I felt bad for myself.

Fuck! Who the hell this guy is now? Why is she hugging him so tight? I thought.

That long hug ended and they separated. I took a sigh of relief. He consoled her. I frowned at him.

'Hey, he is my friend Vardan,' Niti introduced me with them. We shook hands.

'You guys, wait here. I'm going to talk to SHO,' said Samar. We nodded. I just shook my head.

'Who is this guy?' I whispered to Niti as soon as Samar disappeared from there.

'Samar? He is my cousin. I told you *na* I lived at my maternal uncle's place till 12th,' mumbled Niti and I took a deep breath. 'And she is Samar's Fiancé—Ananya,' she added, pointing towards that tall girl. I shook my head, grinning inside.

'Nice couple,' I said, smiling. I was harked back to the situation we were in when I found her not smiling back. I cleared my throat.

Niti explained everything to Ananya till Samar came back.

'Let's go,' said Samar as he came back. He marched towards the exit door. We followed him.

'These assholes take bribe from all the roadside stall owners. This is the reason why they don't take any action against them. I want to slap these fucking evil cops every time I see them,' squealed Ananya as we came out of the police station. She kept screeching and abusing the cops till we sat in Samar's white Fortuner. She seemed a bold girl. Well, I and Niti sat on the back seat.

'I feel burdened picturing that little boy still working at that tea-stall,' mouthed Niti.

Suddenly, I felt like someone put hundred kg weights on my head. I could also feel the burden.

A police siren was heard there. I and Niti turned back. We saw, two police van were following us.

'Why are they following us?' shouted Niti.

'SHO is there in one police van. We're going to that tea stall. Don't we have to rescue the little boy and teach a lesson to that tea-seller who misbehaved with my little sister?' smirked Samar. That smirk was appreciated.

'I love you, *bhai*,' exclaimed Niti. I cheered inside. *I love you Niti's bhai*, I wanted to say.

'He got us out of there…now the SHO is coming behind us… who the hell is your brother?' I whispered to Niti, raising my eyebrows.

'My uncle is an MLA and he is his only son,' she whispered back and winked at me smiling. Her smile was back, finally.

We reached there. SHO whacked the tea-seller over his head before throwing him into the police van. Niti had a word and few moments with that little boy before a children-NGO van came there to rescue him.

'Sir, hope everything is okay now?' said the SHO, wearing back his cap.

'Yes, thank you so much,' replied Samar. They shook hands.

'We will take a leave now. And sir, say good things about me to your father,' murmured the SHO, smiling weirdly. He left.

'Let's get into the car. We have to go to Dibisha's place after dropping you guys, there is a small gathering. They will be waiting for us,' suddenly, shouted Ananya, slapping her head and rushing towards the Fortuner.

'You guys can go to Dibisha's place, I will drop Niti. My car is parked near IIT gate, just walking distance from here,' I interrupted, hesitantly. I wondered *who Dibisha was*.

'Yes, Vardan will drop me. You guys will get late and Dibisha Di will kill you both,' added Niti, laughing. Samar and Ananya joined her. I just maintained a smile on my face.

'Who is Dibisha, by the way?' I mouthed in Niti's ear.

'She is Samar and Ananya's best friend from college,' she whispered back. I nodded and missed my best friends Sejal and Adithya badly. I had a pile of things to share with them now.

16.

After goodbye and cuddling rituals, they left. I and Niti started walking towards the IIT gate. We walked in silence.

'I'm feeling relaxed after the rescue of that little boy,' said Niti, breaking the silence and sitting in the car.

'I can sense that. Well, we have rescued one kid, but nothing is going to change. We see it everywhere; we can't help all the kids. We can't actually change this. And it can also get you in trouble some day,' I said. I sounded like a pessimist, but I wanted to say that since we were at that tea-stall. I drove off and we headed towards her place.

'I know this and I feel really bad sometimes. There is child labor act. Even there is RTE act in our country, according to that every child who is below fourteen years old must go to school. But neither the system nor police care about this. Even no one does. I just try to do what I can do,' she said, sounding extremely disappointed. I shook my head, though it was really heavy for me to hear all that. I felt myself included in her *no one cares* slang. I could care if that was going to help me in getting her in bed.

'Even no one cares I'm still a virgin,' I murmured to myself.

'What?' You said something?'

'No, nothing. I was just saying you're doing something really great,' I mumbled. She smiled and shook her head.

As she was tired, she fell asleep in mid way while talking. We reached her place, but she was still sleeping. I didn't wake her up. I let her sleep and waited for her to wake up. The wait seemed worth watching her sleep peacefully.

She woke up after thirty minutes. I unfastened my seatbelt, removed keys and lifted the handbrake up, acting as if we had just reached there.

'Hey, sorry, I slept off. When did we reach?' She made a tiny yawn.

'It's okay! We have just reached,' I said, helping her unfasten her seatbelt. We got out of the car.

She walked around the car and stood near me. 'Well, sorry for the day, Vardan. You would be wondering what all happened suddenly,' she said.

You're absolutely right, *you're absolutely right,* I thought.

'No, nothing like that. I'm happy that I was a part of some good deed,' I said, smiling. She smiled back.

'You know, I really liked it when you pushed that wicked tea-seller away.'

'I hated the way he yelled at you and came near.'

'Thanks Vardan, for everything,' she said, came close and hugged me. I was surprised. We used to hug, but that was just casual that too for a few seconds. But this one felt different. She hugged me and stayed there for a quite some time. Her head rested against my chest. I put my arms around her and we hugged tightly. We pulled away from each other and kept staring into each other's eyes.

'Good night,' she said. I couldn't hear that as I was still looking into her eyes, lost. I just saw her lips moving. I wanted to put my fingers on her lips to make them stop moving and place my lips on them. I wanted to kiss her so badly.

Kiss her, go ahead, kiss her Vardan, kiss her, a part of me told to myself. But I didn't know what had happened to me, I stood there numb.

'Kiss her loser, kiss her,' this was what resonated in my head.

'Good night, Vardan,' she repeated. It made me regain my senses.

'Good night,' I muttered.

She turned and walked towards her apartment. She unlocked the door and stepped inside. I stood there and kept looking at the door for some time. My phone rang in my pocket and I realized she had gone inside—it was Adithya though.

17.

'You fiasco, you had to kiss her. You turned out to be a big time loser today, Vardan,' Adithya blurted out. He buried his face in couch. He acted crestfallen as if I had an encounter make out with his girlfriend.

Anyway, it was a long, very long day for me. After dropping Niti, I received a call from Adithya and went to Sejal's place. I told them about the whole day. I told them in details about the unexpected events that took place. They listened to me carefully, gulping some beer. I settled with mango juice as I didn't take alcohol. And Adithya blurted out that *you had to kiss her* thing after every five minutes.

'You did a right thing by not kissing her. It could ruin the moment,' shouted Sejal. She had a beer burp.

'It was going to make the moment more interesting. Don't listen to her. She is four pints down... but man! You had to kiss her. You really have disappointed us today,' shouted Adithya, lifting his face out of the couch and gulping some more beer. He went back on hiding his face into the couch. He was good at gulping, but bad at digesting.

'Rain...tea... how romantic... Believe me that hug meant something,' said Sejal.

'What?' I asked.

'That you have made a good space in her heart.'

'So, I'm doing well at this *potential boyfriend* stuff?' I gulped some mango juice and twisted my body.

'You're doing awesome Vardan, I'm so proud of you,' uttered Sejal. Your drunken friends will always be proud of you. But I was happy about it.

'But, I'm not proud of you today… you had to kiss her…' interrupted Adithya, struggling to stand up. He strode across the room towards kitchen, probably, to bring more beer.

'Leave him, he is high today. Well, I guess you should propose her now,' said Sejal, excitedly. She sat cross-legged, smiling and looking at me. As she was drunk, her eyeballs were moving instantly.

'So, you're sure I will get her laid now? I will finally come out of this virginity nuisance?' I said. And I noticed her face expression changed as she heard that, eyeballs stopped moving and eyebrows rose up, making two mountains. I sensed those mountains were about to fall over me.

'Such a jerk! All you boys are the same. You can never think above your underwear, huh,' she shouted loudly. She stood up and sat on other couch. Adithya came with a pint in his hand and collapsed there, chuckling endlessly. He fell on the floor, laughingly. I wanted to kick his ass.

I stood up and marched towards Sejal.

'What's wrong in that if I expect only one thing? Even when I'm trying my best to become like… whatever that potential boyfriend thing. Or you want me to die a virgin?'

'A relationship is more than sex, Vardan,' uttered Sejal, sounding irritated. Confused, I gulped the last sip of mango juice and scratched my ass.

'Guys, stop this sex stuff. Let's talk some real business. Vardan, you should propose her now, before she friend-zones you,' spoke Adithya, softly. Even, that friend-zone word gave me a twitch.

'Now?' I asked, startled.

'Yes,' he said and suddenly snatched my mobile. He dialed Niti's number. I lay down on him, abusing, to get my phone back, but he slid away and put the phone on speaker. Sejal giggled.

'Propose her, propose her,' they both chanted while I heard Niti's caller tune. I wanted to shove cushion in their mouth.

'Hello,' Niti's soft voice was heard. I felt nervous. I wondered what to say. I rubbed my palms against each other.

'Hello,' she repeated. I looked at both the mess creators. They were gesturing me to propose her, showing their teeth and thumb at the same time. They were whispering—*propose, propose, say you like her,* etc.

'Hey, hi,' I said, softly.

'Yes! Vardan. What happened?' she sounded drowsy. I imagined her head resting on a pillow.

'Nothing , I just called to check if you've slept,' I uttered. Adithya and Sejal slapped their head. Adithya hit his head on sofa.

'Yes, I slept Vardan, you're talking to *sleeping-Niti*,' she mumbled. I could sense her smirking with closed eyes. Both of my drunken lizards tried to stop their chuckles. They hadn't given up yet. They were still gesturing me to propose her.

'Good night, see you tomorrow in college,' I said. She said good night and we hung up. I saw Sejal and Adithya groaning at me.

'Loser,' said Adithya.

'Loser,' repeated Sejal. 'Why didn't you propose her?'

'I don't know. I felt as if I'm scared to do that,' I said. I didn't know why I said that. Maybe I was.

'Vardan is scared to propose a girl? The same guy who approaches girls for sex in just one week of dating?' said Sejal and ended giggling. Her sarcasm hurt me. I pulled my hair, frowning at her.

'She is different. And the fact is I'm enjoying all this…I mean being with her,' I mouthed.

'Enjoying? Being dragged to a police station?' asked Adithya.

'Except that part,' I said.

'You're becoming different. And this different is good,' said Sejal.

'This different is called love. Vardan is falling in love,' shouted Adithya. They both started chuckling and laughing endlessly. They clapped each others' hands and fell on the floor.

'This isn't true. You know I don't believe in this love stuff,' I shouted loudly, trying to sound certain about it. But inside my heart I felt feeble when I said that.

'Awww… seems like someone is being thrust into love,' exclaimed Sejal. She moved forward towards me and hugged me. She patted my back, showering me with sarcasm and sympathy both.

'You guys suck,' I said. Adithya jumped on us and we fell on the floor, cuddling. They kept insisting me for next few minutes that I was in love, and I kept resisting.

Later, I decided to sleep over there as I was extremely tired. We ordered pizza, ate that hungrily and watched few episodes of *Friends* before sleeping on the floor.

* * *

Next morning.

'Where were you last night?' my mother shouted back from kitchen as I entered.

'At Sejal's place,' I replied, throwing my car's keys on table.

'Your father was shouting at me. He was asking for your whereabouts,' she said, coming out of the kitchen, pea-basket in her hand.

'Drink and shout? Tell me when he doesn't.'

'He wasn't drunk last night, *beta*.'

'That's interesting,' I said. I went to the kitchen and took out a chilled water bottle.

'What's up with you? Why are you smiling?' she asked, peeling the peas apart and looking at me with suspicion. I was thinking about the last day spent with Niti. I was trying hard to stop my smile from appearing on my face. But, mothers can gauge your mood anyway.

'Nothing. I need to take a shower,' I said and marched towards my room.

18.

Two weeks later

'Happy birthday, Niti,' I wished loudly over the phone as the longer and the shorter hand met at 12 on the clock.

Since that long day, Sejal and Adithya kept pushing my ass to Propose Niti. And I didn't know what was holding me back. I was just waiting for the right moment or maybe I was scared to lose her. Well, I came to know about her upcoming birthday and decided to propose her on her birthday. I had planned I would go to her apartment with birthday cake at night, would surprise her and then propose her. But my bad luck, in the evening just few hours before her birthday, she told me that she was going to her uncle's place and would stay there. So, thwarted, I settled with becoming the first person to wish her over the phone.

'Thank you so much, Vardan…so, you knew…hmmm… And this is why you have been talking to me over the phone for last thirty minutes, inducing me how better is *Marvel* than *DC*…,' she said. I could sense her grinning. Well, I'd been a *Marvel* fan—also, I didn't know what to talk about for long thirty minutes, impatiently waiting to wish her.

'Yes, I knew and I wanted to be the first one to wish you,' I said.

'And you did it well. You really made me happy,' she said. I could sense her smile. I was glad to make her happy on her special day.

'Did I?'

'Of course, it means a lot to me. Well, Vardan, now I should go. Samar and others will be wondering with whom I'm talking to this long,' she said before I could respond.

'Okay, but listen… today is your big day and I want to make it special. I want to celebrate your birthday… a good place, tall cake, mouth-watering food and an unforgettable company…,' I ended mumbling and grinning. I had thought that I would book any good café and throw a party for her. But I was imagining only two people there in the party.

She laughed. I wondered which part made her laugh, *cake, food or the company...or my whole idea*?

'Okay, Vardan, but make sure, you're going to arrange a tall and large cake, as big as you can,' she said while laughing. I couldn't get her large-cake-joke. 'And I should go now,' she added. Anyway, I jumped in my bed as I heard the word *okay*. I settled down realizing I was yet to propose her.

'Sure, and happy birthday once again.'

'Thanks! See you tomorrow,' she said and we hung up.

Next morning, I called her by nine. She answered the call with a yawn.

'So, the birthday girl is still sleeping,' I said, turning my side in bed.

'Hmmm… just woke up by your call… you woke up this early today?'

I could barely sleep last night, I wanted to say.

'Yes, just woke up and thought to ask you about the plans for the day,' I said.

'Vardan, I call you later,' she said and disconnected the call. I wondered what happened that she disconnected suddenly. *Did I say something wrong? Was I not supposed to wake her up this early on her birthday*? Well, I waited for her call. And around, after an hour I received a Whatsapp text.

`Hi! Vardan. Sry, I hd to discnnct sddnly as my uncle n aunty came to wish me`, she wrote. This text gave me some real peace.

`It's ok. I knew there would be smthing that u hd to disconnct sddnly. Well, I hd to remind u abt my plan`, I wrote back mentioning a wink emoji.

She sent me a laughing emoji. Chat window showed her as *typing*…

`So, u still stick to that… Ok, then don't frget abt the cake`. She mentioned a blushing emoji. This wasn't the right time to tell her what I was sticking at.

So, this cake thing is a serious stuff. Big cake…? Is there going to be a whole bunch of people? I thought. A feeling of disappointment ran through my blood sensing the plan wasn't going to work the way I had expected.

`Don't worry, I have arranged that. And we'll go to a cafe in Hauz Khas`, I wrote mentioning my favorite wink emoji.

`No, Vardan, not there. I'll meet you in Patel Nagar. By two o'clock. I'll take you to a good place.`

'WHAT THE FUCK!!! I have already booked a whole café there,' I mumbled looking at the wall. I went back on texting, realizing the wall wasn't going to answer me.

`Okay, sure, as you say... after all it's your special day,` I wrote her back, with moping face. I called the café to cancel the booking. I ordered a big-ten-kg cake, to be delivered at an unknown place—somewhere near *Patel Nagar*.

19.

I had parked my car near Patel Nagar metro station, waiting for her. And finally, she appeared after fifteen minutes. She wore a beige-maroon Punjabi Patiala suit. She looked like a princess. Then I saw both her hands were occupied with polythene bags filled with stuffs. I hurriedly sprayed perfume on my black shirt and got down.

'Wow, you're looking beautiful. Happy birthday,' I said as she reached near the car.

'Thanks, Vardan,' she said and lifted her shoulders up, to exhibit bags in her hands.

'Oh! What's in it?' I said, opening the back door of car. I took those bags from her hands and threw them on the back seat.

'Chocolates and snacks,' she said panting. 'Just wait for a while, Wimp is also coming,' she said as she sat on the front passenger seat.

'So, the big cake, a lot of chocolates and snacks—all for her? Justified though,' I smirked. She smirked back.

'See, it's my birthday. Promise me you're not going to pull her leg today,' she announced, grinning.

'As you say. By the way, where are we going? In a public park?' I sulked.

'Here she is,' she shouted, spotting Wimp stroll towards us.

'Careful,' shouted Niti as Wimp sat on the back seat.

'Hi! Vardan,' exclaimed Wimp, offering her hand to me. She looked extremely happy to sit in my car.

'Hello! Well, it's her birthday,' I said and we shook hands.

'I know. I know. I have brought a gift for her too…hi, Niti, happy birthday,' she shouted, leaning forward to hug Niti. They cuddled excitedly and I felt my car shaking.

'Where is Adithya?' asked Wimp, settling down on the back seat.

'And also your best friend Sejal,' added Niti. I had told her about Sejal, a lot of times.

'They both are on the way. Have to tell them the exact location, but only after I come to know first,' I uttered.

Niti smiled. I drove off and she started guiding me the direction, still not revealing the place we were going to, as if it was my birthday and she had something surprising for me.

After ten minutes of driving, I had to push the brake suddenly in front of an orphanage when she asked to stop.

'Now? Left or right?' I asked puzzled.

'We have reached,' she said, looking towards the orphanage through window.

'So, we're going to celebrate your birthday here?' interrupted Wimp. I wished Niti said *no*.

'Yes,' said Niti and got out of the car. Wimp followed. I rested my head on steering, disappointed by the complete failure of my plan.

I imagined few orphans pull my hair while proposing Niti. I parked my car and got down. Few poor kids ran towards us as we entered that orphanage. They all jumped over Niti to hug her. Both the parties looked familiar to each other.

I sent the location to Sejal and Adithya. I saw the whole place was already decorated.

I sat under a tree while Niti and Wimp played with the kids until Sejal and Adithya reached there. It took Wimp just few seconds to become one of those kids. She jumped more than any of them—even when the poor kids made fun of her four large peeping teeth.

'Hey! What a great idea, to celebrate at an orphanage,' uttered Sejal as she along with Adithya walked up to me—her hands on her cheeks and eyes wide open. I didn't know if she was saying it sarcastically or she was serious. But I didn't like it. I frowned at her.

'What's great in that? She is pretty, even hot, she shares the bills, she is a good human being, but now I'm feeling like she is a freak too… otherwise who celebrates their birthday at an orphanage with the poor kids roaming here and there. I had booked a whole fucking café. We could have partied there instead of giggling and jumping with these poor kids,' I shouted frustrated. I was really disappointed.

'Easy, easy… Can you stop acting like a jerk, Vardan? Trust me I have never heard something great than this. Look how happy she is, what else matters?' she took a pause and looked at me. She continued seeing me not answer *what else mattered*. 'Let's try to make her day more special. And introduce me to her first,' whispered Sejal. I glared at her. Adithya chose to be quiet. I could sense him chuckling, covering his mouth.

Niti saw Adithya and walked to us. Wimp ran behind her, with few kids. I maintained a fake smile on my face.

I introduced Sejal to Niti and Wimp. They shook hands. Adithya and Sejal wished Niti. Kids giggled looking at us, I didn't know why.

'Vardan keeps talking about you,' said Niti to Sejal. A kid held Niti's right hand and started to hover. I held Niti, sensing she could fall. I glared at that kid and he ran away giggling.

'Same pinch, even he keeps talking about you,' said Sejal and smiled. Adithya chuckled. Wimp giggled and I looked other way.

Girls gossiped for a while and went back on playing with those kids. Adithya went to join them when Sejal and Wimp called us. I chose to sit under the tree, figuring out now how and when I will propose Niti.

The kids clapped when the big-cake arrived there. Niti looked at me smiling. A guy who worked at that orphanage came with cold drinks and some more snacks. I saw Niti paying him money.

Later, everyone gathered and waited for Niti to cut the cake. I stood beside her.

We all started singing *happy birthday to you*...as she blew the candles off and cut the cake. She cut a piece of cake and gestured to feed me first. I liked that gesture.

Kids attacked on the balloons. Wimp and Adithya joined them. Sejal and I were cutting the cake into pieces when Niti helped orphanage people to put the snacks on plate.

'Keep quiet you little monsters and stand in a queue,' I yelled at the kids who were scuffling and pushing each other to grab the cake first.

'Don't shout at them, Vardan. They are little kids, they just want some love,' shouted Niti, coming towards us.

'They need some cake I guess,' I said. Niti caressed the kids, assured them that they all would get the cake and then helped me in distributing the cake pieces to them. They took it and ran away leaping.

20.

After the little party, we all presented out gifts to Niti. Most of the kids had presented hand-made gifts.

Few of the kids danced and cracked some jokes for Niti when the other ones clapped continuously. I was sitting alone on a bench at a distance, but I could see and hear all of them. And then, all the kids gathered and sang a song for Niti together. I saw Niti was extremely happy, she was almost blushing.

For a moment I thought myself as a big asshole for thinking just about my plans, thinking about proposing her only when my first concern should have been to make her happy. I thought maybe all of this was better than my plan.

She came and sat beside me.

'Hey, why are you sitting alone? Aren't you enjoying?' asked Niti.

'No, not like that. I'm enjoying seeing you happy. Seriously,' I said looking at her.

'Yes, I really am. Very Much. These kids make my day,' she said.

'Thanks for the cake by the way,' she added.

'It's fine. That was the little I could do for you,' I said.

She smiled. So did I. We both smiled and then fell silent for next few seconds.

'Can you see that little girl?' suddenly, she asked, breaking the silence.

I looked around for the little girl. I saw there was a girl standing at a distance in our right.

With her messy hair scattered all around her shoulders, having a balloon in her right nose and surging mucus in left, she was holding a cold drink glass in both her hands tightly.

'Yes. She needs a hanky to clean her nose. And she also needs to take a shower immediately,' I mumbled, smirking.

'Vardan,' she dabbed my shoulder. I chuckled.

'Can you see the smile on her face?'

I saw. The little girl was smiling. I didn't know why. I just nodded.

'This is the best thing I like about these kids. Their future is completely uncertain. They don't have parents to love them. They are deprived of many privileges as a child, but they never complain. They just never fail to smile,' she said, looking constantly at that little girl.

What is the best thing you like about me? At some point, I'm also underprivileged—I'm still a virgin when most people of my age are not. I too need some love and attention, a part of me thought. When another part of me thought sincerely about what she had just said. I felt bad about that fact.

'You are like an angel for these kids,' this is what I could say in between my thoughts.

She smiled. 'You know what my mother used to call them little angels. She used to visit here regularly. She was the one who started celebrating my birthday here. That's why I always come here on my birthday. I feel like she is standing right beside me,' she said and felt quiet suddenly. She looked the other way.

I hunted for words, but I couldn't find one that could console her. We sat in silence for a moment.

'You know what wherever is your mother she would be really proud of you today,' I said, looking up at the sky. I really meant that.

'Thanks,' she said. Others joined us there before I could say more.

We stayed in that orphanage for a next few hours. Niti distributed some clothes to the kids which she had already arranged.

We walked out. Sejal said she would drop Wimp and Adithya and winked at me. They hugged Niti, said goodbye and left.

I and Niti sat in my car and I drove towards her home. We were silent. We didn't talk much. She played her favorite tracks during our journey while I kept thinking that I should propose her today or not.

We reached her place and got out of the car. She walked a bit and stood in front of me.

'Thank you Vardan, Thank you so much for everything. Thank you for being there and making my day more special,' she exclaimed and looked into my eyes. Her face beamed. I too looked into her eyes, but I didn't utter a single word. I wasn't even blinking, was just looking at her constantly. My hands moved and held her hands in mine. Then she moved closer and hugged me, her hands around my shoulders. That regained my senses. I put my hands around her waist. We hugged. We hugged tightly. I tightened my grip as if I never wanted that hug to end. After a few seconds, she removed her hands and tried to move away. But I didn't want to. I let my hands rest around her waist. She lifted her head up and looked at me, her hands on mine—

trying to remove them from her waist. Confused, she shook her head up, staring at me. I didn't say anything. I just tried to pull her closer. Then I crawled up my right hand to her neck, left hand still on her waist.

I gently placed my right hand on her left cheek, moved my head forward and put my lips on hers. She closed her eyes. Electricity ran through my blood as my lips met with hers. I turned around while kissing her, pushed ourselves against my car and leaned over her. My hands moved around her neck. I was kissing slowly. Those were the softest lips in the world. For next few seconds I kept running my lips over hers. But she wasn't responding. She wasn't kissing the way I was doing.

I felt to stop and ask her if she wasn't comfortable with it. But then I felt her responding. I felt she started running her lips. I got filled with rejoice. But the very moment was just for two or three seconds as she pushed me away suddenly.

'Stop it Vardan,' she screamed. I looked at her surprised and shocked. She looked blank. She had hid her emotions to appear on her face. She ran her hands through her hair. I stood beside, looking at her incessantly. She looked other way. For next few minutes, we didn't utter anything. I didn't know what to say. I put my hand on her shoulder. She shrieked and inched away to remove my hand out of her shoulder. She started marching towards her door.

'Niti, I'm sorry… I just… I mean…' I hunted for words, tramping behind her. I kept repeating sorry stuff, but she didn't give a fuck to that. She unlocked her door and entered. I placed my hands on the door before she could close it.

'Hey, listen… please… we need to talk. I need to explain,' she cut me off, slapping the door on my face as if saying *fuck off*. I didn't know what I would explain to her had she waited to listen, but I felt terribly bad that she didn't. Abruptly, I felt like I did a big mistake of kissing her. I felt like I lost her. I sat in front of her door, realizing that just few minutes back I had the most amazing kiss of my life, even when it was one sided and the shortest kiss I had ever had.

Disappointed, I drove towards home.

* * *

'See, your useless prince has just arrived,' shouted my father as I entered. He lobbed the whiskey glass on table. My mother came out of kitchen.

'Come here and sit. I need to talk to you,' he added.

I just marched towards my room, leaving him blabber.

My mobile beeped as I shut the door of my room. I hurried to get my mobile out of my pocket, expecting a text from Niti.

It was a text from Sejal, `Did you propose her?`

I threw my mobile on my bed.

21.

'Hey, I have been waiting for you for last one hour. I need to talk,' I followed her catching my breath as she marched towards the classroom.

I could barely sleep last night. I spent my night walking in my room and switching sides in bed.

What if I hurt her?

What if she never talks to me now?

What if she abuses and punches me in the face?

What if she says fuck off asshole don't talk to me? Such harrowing thoughts kept resonating in my head and didn't let me sleep.

Next morning, I reached college earlier and waited outside for Niti. I tried talking to her as soon as she appeared, but she didn't pay any heed. She just stomped her feet towards the classroom.

She entered to the classroom. I followed. She sat with Wimp and I sat with Adithya.

'Hey asshole, happy to see you alive. Where the fuck have you been since last night that you didn't respond my calls and texts?' whispered Adithya as I sat down. I didn't respond him. I was looking at Niti.

'Okay leave that and tell me, did you propose her or not?' he added, nudging and guffawing. I frowned at him instead of responding. He sat back bemused.

'At least talk to me, Niti,' I stood in front of her as we came out of the class after the lecture ended. She gazed at me. I thought she would respond this time, but she didn't. She started walking instead. I wondered if she has forgotten how to speak after that unanticipated kiss.

'What am I supposed to think? Are we never going to talk again now?' I shouted behind her. I felt feeble in my knees scaring what if she says *yes never*.

She stopped and turned back. Few of her hair fell on her face. She didn't care to move them aside. She stared at me. I felt petrified.

'What do you want to talk, Vardan? Do you want to talk about the unexpected kiss? THE VERY FIRST KISS OF MY LIFE, you want to discuss how was it? Good or bad? Want to calculate how well or badly it felt?' she burst out. She finally spoke. She was looking at me exhaling, as if asking for an immediate answer. She removed her hair from face and put them behind her ear.

'No, I just want to say sorry if I hurt you in anyway,' I blurted out. Hands in jeans pocket, I made a face as if I was world's most innocent guy.

She stood silent. I toddled towards her. She started walking. I walked beside her.

'Can we sit and talk? Just talk? Please?' I asked softly as we stopped in the middle of the college field. We sat on the green field. I held her hands.

'I'm really sorry if I hurt you. I never meant to. I don't know what happened suddenly. I thought we had a moment… so… just,' I ended fumbling as she cut me off removing her hand out of mine.

'Stop saying sorry again and again. I think it's my mistake too as I didn't stop it when I could have. I shouldn't have hugged you in the first place,' she took a pause.

Please don't say you're never going to hug me now. Please don't call it a mistake, I thought. I wanted to scream this out. But I didn't.

She continued, 'It's better we never talk about this. Just pretend it never happened. Just make everything as it was before last evening.'

'Or let's keep repeating it again and again and pretend like nothing happened, never happened,' I murmured to myself.

I nodded to what she had said. I pulled out grass leaves out of the ground to release my frustration. I plucked a grass leaf and tore them into small pieces. I counted thirteen pieces of that grass leaves were lying on the ground and one left in my hand. I decided not to reap it anymore to make them fifteen pieces.

'So, you will be like this now?' I asked, looking at her.

She shook her head, 'Like?'

'Like this serious and quiet.'

'It will take some time… to be normal… I guess,' she said and an imp smile sketched on her face.

'Okay, take your time till we reach the cafeteria. Let's go there, my stomach is craving for some food,' I laughed. I laughed alone. I stood up, dusting my ass to remove the dirt out of my denim.

I ordered a grilled cheese sandwich and she settled with lemonade. For next few minutes, I focused on my sandwich only. I took giant bites and gulped them, hardly cared to mince them in my mouth. I was super hungry. The last thing I had eaten was Niti's birthday cake last evening. Then, I lifted my eyes up and noticed that she was staring at me, smiling.

'Actually, I skipped my breakfast today, so,' I muttered, running my mouth.

'It's okay. You can order one more sandwich if you want,' she said and laughed. I would have eaten ten more sandwiches hungrily if that was going to keep her laughing.

Anyway, later we ordered noodles and shared. We sat there for some time, talking, laughing and cracking few lame jokes. Things turned normal before we went back to the class.

* * *

'It was better than I was expecting,' I slurped the cold coffee. After college, I along with Adithya went to Connaught Place to meet Sejal. We sat in Starbucks, N block.

'Otherwise, I was really scared if she would ever talk to me or not,' I added.

'I'm telling you she also has a thing for you,' said Adithya, playing with his mobile.

'Or maybe she just doesn't want to lose her best friend. I don't understand why you didn't propose her,' Sejal took the last sip of her coffee.

'When you had to kiss, you didn't. And when you had to propose, you just jumped over her and sucked her lips,' added Adithya. I stared at him as I didn't like his *sucked her lips* slang. He smirked weirdly.

'I didn't know what had happened to me. It was like I had a moment and I couldn't resist to kiss her,' I gave explanation to my two unofficial relationship experts. We came out of the Starbucks and started walking around.

'Well, you never cared about any girl before that she would talk to you or not, then why were you worried and scared this time? I guess you're completely in love with her. You should let her know before it's too late,' she mumbled, looking at me.

'I agree,' said Adithya. I didn't deny nor agreed. I just kept walking with them.

'But you're lucky. You got to kiss her before even proposing her,' he stopped to grin. 'You know, I got my first kiss with Khushi (his girlfriend) after dating her for long six months,' he ended giggling.

'And you know what I have made thirteen girls naked and I'm still a virgin. So, a kiss isn't a big deal for me. You should know,' I mumbled angrily. I wasn't very much proud of that. I just said that thing in a moment of rage. And I lied about that it wasn't a big deal to kiss Niti. It surely was. I couldn't forget about it since the time I kissed her.

'Cut the bullshit. I'm with you, jerks,' shouted Sejal. I and Adithya chuckled. 'Stop chuckling and drop me home. I have some unfinished project work,' she added.

'If thinking of her all the time and having a fear of losing her is called love then *I'm in love with her*. I surely am,' I told to myself while driving back to home.

22.

Three days passed; continuing to gawk at her during lectures, hanging around with her after college, feeling content that I was really in love with her; this time from the bottom of my heart not from the bottom of my zip, going over and over what I would say to her, and terrifying myself about her reaction after realizing that how much I loved her and how eagerly I wanted to hold her hand.

I was in class, sitting on my bench, clutching a pen in my right hand in lap, squinting at Niti doggedly, and mulling over the thought that said *you have to tell her today what you feel for her you have to tell her today*. She was busy in scribbling her notes as the Prof. lectured.

'Many of my doubts got cleared today,' she mumbled, shoving her notebook in bag and stepping out of the class. I walked beside her.

'Yes, it was a nice class. Indeed,' I said. Even though I hardly noticed what took place in the class.

'Nice for you too? I don't think you were concentrating as you were looking around whenever I looked at you,' she said, smiling. She ran her hands through her hair to tie them behind, holding a clip between her lips.

'I don't have to concentrate when I know you're going to scribble every single word, scratched on white board by the professor, in your notebook,' I said, laughing. She laughed along. Abruptly, I stopped laughing, realizing that I had to confess her about something very serious today. I felt suffocation inside my heart. I felt like someone was choking my throat and pulling me back. I realized how easy it used to be for me to say *I love you* before. But I couldn't understand this resistance.

I cleared my throat to speak. 'Hey, I wanted to tell you something,' I said. I felt stupid to utter like that. There was a romantic scene going on in my head, all like it happened in Bollywood movies; where the male lead proposes to the female lead on their knees.

She laughed. I wondered why. *Did she hear me out talking to myself?* I thought. I shrugged my shoulders.

'Even I was about to say the same thing… wanted to tell you something,' she said between the laughter. I wondered if she would laugh the same way after I tell her what I was going to confess.

'And that is?' I asked, stroking my chin.

'I won't be coming to college for next three days.'

'WHAT???' I shouted surprisingly. 'I mean why?' I added, sensing the awkwardness of my tone.

'I'm going to Chandigarh.'

'Chandigarh?'

'Yes, I have an early morning train tomorrow. There is an NGO that works for underprivileged students. They conduct sessions in different cities across the country and help such students achieve their educational goals and motivate them. I will be volunteering with them,' she said. I was choked. I felt to gather all the underprivileged students of this country and hurl them somewhere very far that she could never reach them and spend all her time with me. I had no idea what to say then.

'What happened?' she shook me through my shoulder and broke the awkward silence there.

'Nothing. So, next three days?' I uttered.

'Yes. But it can be five too as I'm planning to visit my Nani's place.'

'Your maternal grandparents live there?'

'Fifteen kilometers from the railway station,' she said and I nodded.

'You wanted to tell something?' she said. I changed my plan and thought I would tell her when she comes back.

'Nothing. I was just planning to go for a movie together,' I mumbled, faking a smile. Later, I helped her in shopping; she had to buy things for the students.

Next morning. I reached college. She wasn't around as expected. I tried to concentrate in class, but I couldn't. I was just staring at the empty seat where she used to sit; I realized how much I missed her and how difficult it was to be there without her. I couldn't hold on to the uneasiness for a long and left the class after first lecture. Adithya walked behind me.

'What happened?' he asked, putting his right hand on my shoulder from behind.

'Nothing,' I replied, looking at my mobile screen, to check if any text was received from her. Her last seen was from last night, she didn't come online today.

Hey, where are you? I typed a text for her, but deleted without sending.

'Why did you leave the class suddenly? What's the matter with you?'

'It's Niti,' I murmured, folding my hands and looking around.

'What Niti? And why didn't she come today? Wait, is she okay?'

'She is, I guess,' I said. I told him about her thing with the underprivileged students and her trip to Chandigarh.

'So, what's wrong with that? She would come back after three days. Or she has asked you for the proxy attendance and you're wondering how to arrange a pair of breasts and a wig to do that?' he ended chuckling. I wasn't in mood to appreciate his chuckle. I glowered at him.

'Moron. It's about…. I'm not feeling good that she isn't around,' I shouted.

'I got it now. The drawbacks of falling in love, not falling, you're probably flying high in love,' he smirked weirdly.

'Flying high,' I mouthed.

'What?'

'Nothing. I'm going,' I said, looking at my Gshock wrist watch. It showed 11:15am.

'Going? Where?'

'Going to Chandigarh,' I said. 'Take these keys, drop me to the airport and park my car at my place.' I threw the keys at him. I rushed into the class, took our bag and notebooks, and came out at a fast pace.

'What will I tell to your mother if she asks me about your whereabouts?' he shouted running behind as I rushed towards the parking area.

'I will call her on my way,' I said, gasping.

Adithya drove the car. I tried Niti's number on my way to the airport, but it was running *not reachable*. It took me five attempts to get connected with her.

'Hey, I was thinking to go to Chandigarh with you. I too want to be a part of some good cause,' I uttered as soon as I heard her answer the call.

'It's really good to hear, but, Vardan, I'm in the train right now. I have already left,' she said. I could hear rhythmic sound of the running train.

'I will reach there before you, just text me your train details, bye,' I said and disconnected.

'Next flight to Chandigarh please,' I enquired. I was at the ticket counter, IGI airport, Delhi.

'Available for 1:45pm. Which class sir?'

'Business class would be preferred.'

23.

I landed in Chandigarh at 2:50pm. I had to rush to the railway station now. I reached two hours before her train's arrival and waited for her impatiently. Meanwhile, I called my mother and told her that I would be going to Chandigarh for some college project work and would come back after three days.

'WHAT? Why didn't you tell me this earlier? What kind of project you are working on that came so suddenly? Why did your friend Adithya just parked the car and ran away when I asked him about you? What will I answer your father now? And, beta, what will you eat there?' she fired questions at me. This is every mother's prime concern that what will you eat if you're not home. They think you will get nothing to eat when you are outside your home.

'Mom, don't worry, I will eat on time. You get the best food here in Chandigarh. And tell dad I'm going to do some good work. Bye, will talk to you later,' I said and hung up before my mother could fire few more questions.

After I had waited for a long time, she finally appeared. She wore a ripped-blue-denim and a loose-white t-shirt. I ran towards her as she got off the train. We hugged.

'I can't believe you're actually here,' she exclaimed, her eyes wide open and hands on her cheeks. We walked out of the railway station, took a cab and went to the NGO camp she was supposed to visit. It was already evening till then. Niti took a session and I listened to her talking about the importance of education. I loved staring at her. *She is intelligent*, I thought. We met a lot of students there; few of them were in their twenties. I tried to be nice with them, as nice as possible. It was 10pm when we left the camp and went to a Punjabi restaurant for dinner. We were almost exhausted when we reached our hotel. Weariness could be seen on our faces. We decided to sleep and went to our respective rooms. I thought I would propose her finding the best moment and rehearsed few lines before crashing in my bed.

Next morning, we woke up, got ready, had our breakfast and left for the camp. For rest of the day, we were there. I could barely talk to Niti as she was busy in her sessions. It was quite grueling for me, but I was happy that she was around all the time. It was like I had to content myself with love and suffering in silence until the end of the day. We left the camp at around 9pm and strolled towards a nearby restaurant for dinner.

'How was your day? Are you enjoying? Students liked you very much, I saw them reaching out to you again and again,' she said as we reached the restaurant.

Yes, they were happy to eat my brain, pull my hair and pinch in my ass, I thought.

'Of course, I'm enjoying,' I said. The waiter asked for our order as we sat on the sofa. We ordered our food.

'Don't lie, it's on your face that how much you have enjoyed,' she said and laughed. I chose to smile.

'A bit tedious to be honest,' I stopped to grin. 'Actually, it's new for me and I hadn't expected that we would be there for the whole day.'

'Yes, I understand…,' I cut her off before she could complete.

'Well, are we going to spend tomorrow as well in the same way?' I asked, raising my right eyebrow. Waiter came with the food and served it. He left.

'Don't worry. I won't make it a punishment for you. Tomorrow, we will leave the camp early and visit few nice places as it's your first time in Chandigarh,' she said, smiling. *It's my first time in love too,* I thought. We finished our food and went back to the hotel. I don't remember when I slept as I was too drained to think or do anything but sleep.

* * *

'You know, I try to come here every year, if possible. I have so many memories attached to this place. I still remember I was five when I visited this place for the first time with my mother, Nana and Nani. Sometimes I feel like settling down here, a small home surrounded by hundreds of students and this lake,' she exclaimed. We were at the Sukhna Lake, strolling around on the pathway. Our third day in Chandigarh; we left the camp in the afternoon, visited Rose garden, and then went to Sukhna lake.

'At least ask me before planning to settle down anywhere,' I murmured to myself.

'It's really a beautiful place. I would love to visit here again… with you,' I ended mumbling. She smiled.

'Thanks for coming here. Even for coming to Chandigarh,' she said. I looked in her eyes. 'Hey, you want to try boating,' suddenly she shouted before I could say something.

I would like to try anything and everything with you, I thought. We did boating together, it was fun. We strolled around the lake for quite a time and left for Elante Mall.

'Do you have to buy something?' I said on our way to the mall.

'Yes, I have to buy something for my grandparents. I will be going to their place tomorrow morning. Well, have you booked your tickets back to Delhi?'

'You will go… how long will you stay there?' I said, my voice faltered. I expected her to say *I would stay there just for one hour and then would go back to Delhi with you.* I wished she could hear my silent screams.

'I guess at least for two days as I'm visiting them after one year, almost,' she said. I nodded. I felt my legs shake in disappointment.

'You came alone you will go back alone, Vardan,' I murmured to myself.

She bought whatever she needed from the mall and we came back to the hotel. She went to her room and I went to mine. I sat on my bed, thwarted. I started scolding myself for spending three days with her and not even proposing; now I had to pack my bags to go back to Delhi, *alone*. I kept sitting on bed, scolding myself, for next one hour. I didn't even move. Then suddenly, I stood up and went in front of the mirror. I started uttering the things I had been rehearsing for last two nights. I decided to go to her room and spit out everything that I had gathered for her inside my heart. I went over and over on what I had to say to her, before going to her room.

24.

I stood outside her room for a while, preparing myself before pushing the door half open. I stepped my right leg inside the room, held on the door and looked around to find her. I saw she was standing in front of her temporary dressing table, staring herself in the mirror, and holding an earring near her right ear; probably to check if that matched with her dress or not. She was wearing a Saree and backless blouse. She hadn't noticed me enter till then, as she was busy staring herself in the mirror and selecting the earrings. I entered the room. She turned startled as she heard the door shut.

'DAMN!!! God, why did you make this girl so beautiful?' this is what I murmured to myself, gauging her from head to toe, when she turned and my eyes fell on her. Red silk Saree with blue georgette threads used along with the golden silk threads and blue-deep-neck-fitting blouse, she looked the most beautiful girl in the world or any other world existed or the whole galaxy. I gazed down, toned skin of her slim stomach was visible, and half of her navel peeped behind her Saree *pallu*. She looked ravishingly seductive.

I noticed she wasn't wearing her left earring, it was on the table. Anyway, I kept checking her out until she interrupted.

'Hey, you startled me. Well, I was about to come to your room, to show you my Saree-look. Then stopped to wear my earrings,' she stopped to grin, her hand on her breast, holding her breath. She continued, 'Well, how am I looking?'

'Voluptuously hot,' I mouthed. I gaped at her, drooling.

'What?'

'You're looking gorgeous,' I uttered, mouth still open. I shut my mouth and gulped the water gathered all around my jaw.

She chuckled, blushing, 'Thank you.' She turned back to the mirror. I toddled towards her, slowly.

'Tomorrow, I will be wearing this Saree while going to my Nani's place. She loves seeing me in Saree. So, was just checking and also, wanted to show you my Saree-look,' she mumbled looking in the mirror. I stood just behind her, gazing tenderly. I badly wanted to touch her bare back, wanted to hold her from behind and kiss her nape, but I didn't, harking back to the reason I had invaded into her room. She wore her left earring. I looked up into the mirror, our eyes met and she smiled. She turned her side and we looked at each other. I looked into her eyes. I forgot every single line I had rehearsed. I stood there dumb and naïve, fixing my eyes on her constantly. She kept looking more and more beautiful every single second passed.

Perplexed, she uttered, breaking the awkward silence in the room, 'What happened, Vardan?' I felt like her lips were moving in slow motion.

I moved an inch forward, close to her. 'Niti, can I ask you something?' I almost whispered. I just said it, but, at that moment, I didn't even know what I was going to ask her for. And then, my hands moved towards her hands, slowly, and the next moment, her hands were in mine. I held them gently.

'Yes, what's that?' she said, her voice dropped with every next word she had uttered.

'CAN I GET FIFTEEN MINUTES OF YOUR LIFE?' I said, looking straight into her eyes, her hands still in mine. She looked into my eyes, puzzled.

She didn't say *yes*. Nor did she say *no*. She just didn't say anything. I considered her answer as—*yes*. Abruptly, I heard my own heartbeat as if it wanted to scream something.

Heart,

This is the right time. Say her. Tell her that how much you love her. Vardan, just keep your heart out today. This is the exact moment you have been waiting for days.

I was just about to utter what was in my heart for her, and then, my mind interrupted.

Mind,

Vardan, you're just a few inches away from her. Pull her close, hold her tight and kiss every inch of her skin. She is gorgeous, attractive and voluptuously hot. Just place your lips on hers, and if you stand lucky you can get laid today, with this ravishingly beautiful girl.

I tried to ignore whatever was leaping in my mind and decided to focus on my heart, but, unfortunately, my eyes were with my mind. My eyes couldn't resist ogling at her perky breasts; impatiently trying to jump out of her deep-neck-fit blouse, and beautifully carved navel; peeping out of her Saree pallu.

After a few seconds of combat in between my heart and mind, I placed my right hand on her waist and pulled her close. I got goose-bumps when my fingers touched the bare skin of her waist.

25.

'What are you doing, Vardan?' she mumbled. I snubbed her gripe. I felt her warmth. I slinked my left hand up through her hand slowly and gently moved my fingers around her neck and behind ear. She sighed reluctantly.

I grabbed her waist tightly, craned my neck forward and put my lips on hers. I started kissing her slowly. She didn't part her lips to kiss back, but I didn't stop. I kept kissing her soft pink lips while my hands moved around her neck and waist.

All of a sudden, she pushed me away, wheezing. I looked at her, she was looking down. For next few seconds, we didn't move. Stood there like zombies. She gestured to say something, but, before a single word could fall out of her mouth, I went near her and whispered.

'Twelve minutes are still left,' I spoke softly and held her in my arms, without letting her respond. I shove my face in her shoulder and ran my lips around her neck. I started giving pecks all over her face, her eyes close. And then, her pallu fell out of her shoulder, leaving her cleavage uncovered. My eyes doubled its size as I ogled there. She tried to put her pallu back in place, but I held her hand.

She turned other way and yelled, 'It's wrong, Vardan. Please stop all this.'

I held her from behind and pushed ourselves against the wall. Her pallu fell on the floor.

'It doesn't feel wrong… it doesn't feel…,' I mumbled while putting my lips on the center of her neck. I hugged her tightly from behind, as tight as possible, while kissing all over her neck. Then I brushed her hair aside to her left shoulder and kissed on her back. Grudgingly, she heaved a sigh. I snaked my hands all over her belly and circled my right hand fingers around her belly button. Her skin felt as soft as silk.

My hands crawled up and reached her breast while I kept kissing on her back. My right hand could feel her cleavage. She put her hands on mine and tried to remove them from there. But till then, she also knew that resistance was just futile now. She removed her hands from there and I groped her breast in my hands. She sighed heavily when I pressed them gently. I could hear her breathing deeply. I turned her side, her eyes closed. I unhooked two buttons of her blouse and buried my face there. It turned me on even more. I ran my mouth there rapidly as if I wanted to eat them. She ran her hands through my hair, breathing heavily. She caught my hair tight as if she wanted to pull them out of their roots.

I removed her blouse and felt like losing my sense by seeing her in cherry red bra. It was extremely seductive. She looked astoundingly hot. I cuddled her tightly. She buried her face in my chest. I could feel her lips there.

I removed her Saree before pushing her gently on the bed. I leaned over her, removing my t-shirt. I put my lips on her head and went down kissing. I locked my lips with hers. It turned me more excited when I felt her responding. I just increased the speed of kissing. For next some time, we kept kissing and stopped to gasp some oxygen.

I came down and kissed around her belly. She moaned heavily when I kissed on her belly button, both her hands held on the bed sheet. I looked up, her eyes close, she bit her lower lip and struggled to hide the sensation she was going through. But, she couldn't resist moaning back when my tongue played impishly with her navel.

She moaned heavily when I placed my lips on her thighs. I crawled up on her thighs kissing and held on both the corners of her panty to pull it down. I stopped to look at her. She opened her eyes and glimpsed at me. She was looking at me constantly, without even a single blink. There was lust as well as hate in her eyes. The lust unexpectedly evoked by me was going to last just for few minutes, but the hate was going to last forever. I looked deep down in her eyes, but no sign of love was found. We were almost naked, she was too near to me, but yet, it felt like she had gone too far from me. And the battle between my heart and mind started again.

Heart,

Are you sure this is what you actually want?

Mind,

You have been waiting for this moment for a very long, very long Vardan. What else you want lying naked next to her?

Heart,

Did you come here for this? You came here to tell her that you love her. Did your desperation go over your love? Or you don't love her? You just want her body? You just want to use her to satisfy your lust?

Mind,

Don't think much. Just pull down the last cloth on her body and go ahead. Enter her. Get her today. Get her.

Heart,

Get her today and lose her for rest of your life.

There was death silence in the room, yet the echo of the conversation between my heart and mind was quite disturbing for me. I saw she placed her hands on her bare breasts and looked away. Suddenly, my hands got removed from her panty. I decided not to go ahead. I stood up and got into my clothes hurriedly. I looked at her, she was still lying like frozen. I wanted to put the Saree on her naked body, but I couldn't gather the courage. I wasn't able to make eye contact with her. I wanted to leave that place as soon as possible.

'THREE MINUTES ARE STILL LEFT,' she screamed as soon as I reached the door. I could sense hearing her voice that how much she hated me in that moment.

'May be, someday I will use these three minutes to tell you that what I actually feel for you,' I said, holding the door and without looking at her.

'I never want to see your face again,' she shouted. She declared.

I left.

* * *

'It's 2am, beta,' whispered my mother as soon as she opened the door. I paid no attention to what she said and entered.

She continued whispering, 'Why have you come this late? And even why did you go there suddenly? You know your father; he has been asking me about your whereabouts for last three days…walk slowly, your father will wake up.'

'I need to sleep, mom,' I said and rushed to my room, without looking at her. I couldn't even make eye contact with my mother.

After leaving Niti's room, I had gone to my room, packed my bag and left for airport. But, before that I wanted to go back to her room, wanted to say her sorry and ask her if I could drop her to her grandparents place. But I didn't have the courage. On my journey back to Delhi, I wanted to call her and apologize to her. Had written sorry-texts and deleted without sending her—multiple of times. As I couldn't gather courage. I was very disappointed and ashamed of myself. The hate I had seen in her eyes was reflecting in front of me again and again. The worst feeling of losing her from my life intentionally was spawning extreme pain and uneasiness within me. The last line she had said was echoing in my head again and again.

26.

I heard my room's door open. It was them; Sejal and Adithya. I was lying in my bed when they entered. I sat up and tried to look normal, but I was too far from being normal. It had been five days since I came back to Delhi from Chandigarh, and I had hardly stepped outside my house. Had almost locked myself in my room.

'What's wrong with you, man? Why is your number switched off for last few days? I have tried calling your number for fucking multiple times,' said Adithya in his fast accent, sitting beside me on the bed. Next day, when I came back from Chandigarh, I had tried calling Niti's number and realized that she had blocked me. She had also blocked me from Facebook, Instagram and Whatsapp. Later, my mobile's battery got exhausted, and I didn't feel like charging it. Well, it was good to see them after a long time.

'Aunty is saying that you're not talking to anyone and also skipping your meals. Are you fine?' asked Sejal. She bent forward and placed her right hand on my forehead, to check if I was fine—maybe I seemed fine on the outside, but I was very far from being *fine* inside. 'For how long you didn't take shower? Man, you're stinking,' she added, shrinking her nose. I took shower the last time in Chandigarh. I couldn't let her smell go out of my body.

'Niti also didn't come to the college for last few days. So, we thought you are still in Chandigarh with her. I told the same thing to Sejal. When Niti came today, I tried to ask her about you. But she didn't respond anything, just ignored my question and walked away,' said Adithya. I looked at him as soon as I heard Niti's name. But I didn't utter anything.

'Will you please say something and let us know what's wrong? Why have you reduced yourself into a big time fiasco?' said Sejal, collapsing on the couch there. They both kept staring at me—impatiently waiting for the answers.

After a few minutes of silence, I uttered, 'I ruined it.'

'Ruined it? What ruined it?' they both shrieked together and looked at me for an immediate answer. I again went to the silent mode, leaving them disappointed.

'Wait...I guess you proposed her and she didn't accept it. And being an asshole, you couldn't take the rejection that's why you're scolding yourself by locking yourself in the room?' muttered Sejal, raising her one eyebrow and craning her neck forward. I kept quiet and wished it was true what she had assumed. Anyway, I scowled at her. She took her raised eyebrow downwards.

'You messed with her? Or you guys fought? What happened in Chandigarh? Tell us whatever it is. We are your friends,' said Adithya. Sejal nodded. I wondered if I was going to get the same sympathy and support after I tell them my way of proposing Niti.

They kept insisting me to tell them the mess I had created and I just kept quiet—wondering what to tell them. But I couldn't hold on the resistance for a long and told them everything. I told them how I messed my big chance of proposing Niti. I told them how I kept my lust before my love. And I told them how I stopped before ruining everything.

After twenty minutes of silence,

'I have seen you whimpering for only one thing since we met and when you were just one step away from that, you stopped...? Are you kidding me? How could you even stop in that moment? Or you got pre-ejaculation???' he took a pause to grin. 'And you have locked your ass here in disappointment because you're left a virgin once again?' he ended, smirking. I wanted to punch his face very hard that he could never smirk again. *This is not funny, you dickhead*, I wanted to scream. I frowned at him. He sat back and stopped grinning.

And suddenly, Sejal burst out, 'I can't believe all this crap. I'm wondering how she would have been feeling after all this shit...? Disgusting,' she stopped, rubbed her left hand palm on her forehead and continued, 'Being a girl I can say this is the worst thing she would have gone through. You jumped on her like a dog jumps seeing a piece of chicken. You claim that you love her??? Seriously???' she glared at me. I looked away. I felt embarrassed and humiliated.

'Dude, can you please stop your feminism for a while? And what the fuck you're talking about? Can't you see that he is not doing well?' shouted Adithya, looking at Sejal. He stood up.

'You can't support him on this I'm telling you. What's her mistake? Why Niti has to suffer all this? Just because she trusted him?' Sejal yelled back. I got that I wasn't going to take shower for few more days now. I had hung my head down.

'He is not at mistake alone. He felt her seductively attracted and initiated something. Tell me why didn't she stop him? Why did she kiss back? Why did she let him take her clothes off?'

'Because she wanted to see the worst side of him and he showed well...,' Sejal took a pause and continued, 'Or maybe, she also had a thing for him.'

Sejal's last line was like a drop of water for me when I was writhing thirsty for days.

'Whatever. You can't deny the fact that he stopped when it was impossible to stop. He stopped when they were all naked and he was just one step away from entering her. And it takes a lot of will for a boy to stop in that moment. I'm a boy and I know this,' mumbled Adithya, staring at Sejal.

'We were still wearing our last clothes,' I interrupted. But none of them paid heed to that. They were busy in staring at each other.

'Yes, and he must be given a bravery award. He has set a nice example of being courageous,' said Sejal. Her sarcastic dig hurt me.

'Why are you guys fighting?' I said. They both turned to look at me. 'I know I have done something terrible and I'm really ashamed of that.' I felt Sejal would shout *yes, yes, you asshole, you must be ashamed of what you did*. But she didn't.

Adithya came and sat beside me. Sejal remained stood and silent.

'See, forget everything. It's enough now, enough with this virgin thing. Now you will get laid no matter what. Rehaan has sent me few pictures. He told me these girls are first timers, they just charge few more bucks,' he whispered, showing me few pictures in his mobile. He was still thinking that I was upset because I couldn't get laid with Niti like my last thirteen girlfriends.

He started zooming a picture and uttered, 'She is extremely hot... look at her curves, dude. You know she is just eighteen years old. You should choose her.' I fumed inside as much as he zoomed in the picture. And I don't know what happened to me suddenly; I snatched his mobile and threw that hard on the wall. His mobile broke into pieces before falling on the floor. Sejal and Aditya turned to look at the wall, astonished.

It's not that I couldn't get laid with her, it's something else you moron, it's something else, I wanted to scream. But I couldn't.

'*Bhenchod*, what the fuck did you just do? What did my mobile do to you?' screeched thwarted Adithya. He stood up and ran towards the wall. He collected the pieces of his mobile in his hand.

'My girlfriend had gifted me this mobile,' he uttered, sobbing and glaring at me. I was still fuming and frowning at him. Sejal was confused what and how to react. But I knew that she wanted to laugh like anything and she was controlling.

And then I saw my mother pushing the door half open. My mother peeped inside, holding on the door.

27.

'What happened, *beta*?' my mother asked. No one answered for a few seconds.

'Nothing, aunty. Actually my mobile fell from my hand, so...,' unexpectedly, spoke Adithya, faking a smile on his face. I felt bad for breaking his mobile. My mother looked at him for a while, maybe she remembered how he had parked the car and run away without answering her anything last time, and then looked at me. I looked down. She looked at the damaged part of the wall. The wall had got peeled off where mobile hit it. A piece of wall paint was lying on the floor.

'Everything is okay, *beta*?' my mother asked Sejal.

'Don't worry aunty, everything is alright,' uttered Sejal. My mother nodded and left. Sejal shut the door hurriedly.

'I know I did a blunder that she won't even forgive me, but I really love her,' I mumbled. I felt soreness near my throat. I was looking down, my face in both my palms. I was almost crying. They both came on the bed and sat beside me. Adithya put his hand around my shoulder, forgetting that I was the one who broke his mobile few minutes back. I liked his gesture.

'I feel like I lost her,' I added, disappointment in my voice.

'What you did wasn't good, but at least you stopped after realizing your mistake,' before Sejal could complete, Aditya cut her off and said, 'And we're proud of you for the sacrifice you have made for your love.' Sejal stared at him and he fell quiet.

'What next now?' asked Sejal.

'I don't know. But I won't go to the college now,' I said.

'Have you gone nuts? With whom I will sit everyday then?' uttered Adithya. Sejal hit her palm on her head.

'This is your big concern for now?' Sejal yelled, glaring at him. He shrugged his shoulders and looked away.

'What are you talking about, Vardan? Why won't you go to the college?' she asked, furling her hands in the air.

'She doesn't want to see my face,' I paused for a second and continued, 'This is the last thing she said when I was leaving her room. She doesn't want to see my fucking face. Honestly, I also don't know how I will face her.' I took a deep breath.

'She was supposed to say so many bad things to you, she just said this. So, you must be happy about it,' said Sejal and paused. I looked at her face, baffled. She bent forward to grab a pillow. She put that pillow on her lap, placed her elbows on the pillow, rested her chin into her palms and continued, 'Look, she didn't say anything unexpected. Of course, she was mad at you at that time.'

'So, she won't mind seeing his face again?' interrupted Adithya and grinned. Sejal kicked him off the bed.

He crawled up the bed, 'I'm not joking. I'm also serious.'

'He is a rascal. Whatever. What I was saying...yes, forget what she said and remember only one thing that you're yet to tell her that you love her,' said Sejal, looking into my eyes.

'Yes, I agree. She is right. You also have to say her sorry,' uttered Adithya. Sejal looked at him and he shrugged his shoulders. A cold war was going on between them during the whole conversation.

'Go to the college tomorrow and apologize to her. And then tell her what you actually feel for her,' added Sejal.

'You guys think she will listen to me? She will even talk to me?' I murmured, sounding a bit hopeful.

'You have to keep trying until she does. Lying here in your bed like an ass won't help in anything,' said Sejal.

'Yes, bro. You have to fight for you love. You have to tell her,' added Adithya, sounding emotional and furling his fist in air.

Just few hours ago, I was lying hopeless in my bed with a full baggage of disappointment, thinking I lost Niti forever. But their presence and support worked like counseling and made me a bit hopeful now.

'Thank you so much, guys,' I mumbled.

'No matter what, we are always with you,' shouted Adithya and jumped to hug me. Sejal joined. We hugged tightly.

Sometimes I wondered being a big time asshole how did I manage to find such true friends. They were the only ones I had earned in my life till then.

28.

'Let's go for the class. It's already 10am,' said Adithya, sitting in the car and setting his hair in place. Next morning, I had gone to the college and was waiting for Adithya in the parking area before going to the class.

'What happened? Why did you call me here?' he asked, throwing his notebooks on the car dashboard. He looked at me, confused. Without wasting time, I twisted myself left to backside and leaned between the two seats. I lifted a paper bag from the back seat of my car and handed over that bag to Adithya.

'What's this?' he enquired, moving his eyes round. He tried to peep inside the bag.

'Open it,' I spoke softly. He pulled out the gift-wrapped box from that bag and unfolded it inquisitively. His face beamed with delight as soon as he could open that box. I had brought the latest Iphone for him.

'A new Iphone??? Seriously??? It's for me???' he shouted, surprised and smiled with excitement. It felt like he would start dancing in the car as soon as I nodded.

'Thanks, bro,' he said slowly. 'I love you,' he added, moving towards my seat. He hugged me tightly. He seemed really happy. I felt good to see him pleased, after what I had done to his mobile last day.

'Sorry for throwing your mobile like that, I was completely out of my mind,' I said, while hugging him back.

'Bro, it's okay. You can throw this too, but when the next Iphone launches,' he uttered, chuckling and settling back to his seat. I wanted to smile back, but I couldn't. I kept thinking how I would face Niti just after few minutes.

Well, we got out of the car and moved towards the class. I felt unnerved with the every step I took towards the class. Anxiety and nervousness ran through my blood. I wasn't sure how she would react seeing me enter the class. I wasn't sure how I would look into her eyes. I wasn't sure how I would talk to her and if she would even listen to me. And I wasn't sure how I would breathe knowing the fact that the girl I love hates me the most.

We reached the classroom. I stopped at the door and my eyes just moved around to find her frenziedly. She was sitting on her desk with Wimp. She looked at the door and immediately looked away as soon as her eyes recognized my face. The face she never wanted to see again. Colour of her face turned into red. As expected. I felt to run away from there and never come back again. I stood at the door lost, for a few seconds before Adithya held my hand and pulled me inside the class. We sat on our desk. I stared at her from the corner of my eyes. She had hung her head down. She seemed really upset. It seemed like she wasn't mentally present in the class. I missed her scribble down from the whiteboard, talking to Wimp and look at me smiling during the lectures. I missed her happy face. I just wanted to sprint out of the class that she could sit in peace.

'Hey, dude,' suddenly, Rohit and Mohit whispered together. They were sitting behind my desk as usual.

'Where were you for last few days? We really missed your Audi in the parking area,' mumbled Rohit.

'I thought he joined his father's business,' added Mohit. I wasn't in mood to pay heed to their unwanted concerns. I just ignored them.

'He is a Casanova. He would be busy with some new chicks,' uttered Rohit. This hurt me. I hoped Niti didn't hear that.

'Oh, that's why he looks fatigued and exhausted. Seems like he has lost a lot of stamina in last few days,' added Mohit, chuckling slowly. I heard them clapping each other's hands. I wanted to thrash their faces and shove something in their mouth that they couldn't utter anything.

Adithya turned back and whispered, 'Can you both see the pen in his hand? He is hardly interested in using it, but he can easily shove that pen deep into your broad ass. It might be painful. Then you both will look more exhausted. So, better stop spitting the shit out of your mouth, you rascals.'

They both sat back silently.

Anyway, I saw Niti leaving the class with Wimp as soon as the lecture ended. I wanted to stand up and walk behind her to talk to her, but I felt like someone had caught me tight that I wasn't even able to move. I felt like my heart wanted to shout for her name, but my other body parts were not functional. I was scared and frozen. I gained my senses as Adithya shook me up.

'What are you thinking? Go and talk to her, before she leaves,' he whispered, almost pushing me out of our desk. I held on the corner of desk to keep myself from falling on the floor.

'I don't think she will talk to me. She didn't even look at me once,' I mumbled, sounding timidly.

'Why don't you get tired of being an asshole?' he shouted, standing up, and then paused, sensing students sitting near our desk turned to look at us. He bent down and whispered in my ear, 'Talk to her and apologize, this is the only way out. Otherwise nothing is going to change even if you keep thinking about her for thousands of years.'

He looked very confident while saying all that. His valuable advice gave me some courage. I had never thought he would sound that mature and intelligent. I wanted to hug him. But didn't. I rushed out of the class. I looked around and then saw Wimp coming at a distance, throwing her hands in air and talking to herself. I ran to her.

'Where is she?' I asked her, panting.

'Who?' asked Wimp.

'Niti...?'

'Oh, she is in the library. But she is very quiet, looks disturbed… not even talking to me...' I cut her off before she could complete and started walking towards the library.

'No one wants to talk to me,' shouted Wimp.

I entered the library and looked around for her. She was in a corner—sitting all alone. She had hung her head down, head rested on the desk, left hand on books lying on the desk beside her head and right hand on her lap. I moved silently and sat beside her. For next five minutes, I didn't say anything. Or I just couldn't. I had fixed my eyes on her. She wasn't even moving. She was lying on the desk like a body without soul. I wondered if she knew that I was sitting beside her or not.

For that moment, I was almost blank. I didn't know what to say and how to start. I had never thought in my life that I would ever be in such situation.

Somehow, I gathered some courage and whispered, fumbling, 'Hi, Niti. I need to talk to you.'

I waited for her to respond but she didn't even move. I doubted even if she felt my presence there or not.

I continued, 'I know you're extremely angry with me. Possibly you hate me. And you have all the rights to do that after what I did. But please give me one more chance to explain myself. Please talk to me, Niti.'

I was gazing at her without taking a blink. I just wanted her to turn towards me and say something. I wanted her to react anything on what I had said. I wasn't going to mind even if she would abuse me. I just desperately wanted her to talk to me.

After a few minutes of silence,

Suddenly, she stood up. She picked up her books on desk. I thought she would burst out at me. Thought she would shout at me or would hit me from the books in her hand. Thought she would leave no stone unturned to make me realize that how disgusting and a big asshole I was. But she didn't say a single word. Instead she turned her side and started walking. Her silence hurt me deeply.

'Please Niti, talk to me. Please…' I almost begged.

She didn't stop or turn back. She kept walking. She left without even looking at me. For next one hour I kept sitting on that desk frozen. I had turned into a zombie.

Well, this is what I deserved. The girl I loved didn't even want to look at me.

I came out of library toddling, disappointed, drained and exhausted—same like the guy appeared in energy booster drink's ad where sun seemed sucking energy out of his body. And then I saw Divya—my classmate and one of my thirteen ex-girlfriends, walking towards me. She appeared like that energy sucking sun we could see in GluconD ads. I tried to overlook her and walked towards parking area.

'What happened… seems you guys aren't talking?' she blurted out, walking beside me. As I and Niti always hanged out together in the college, everyone thought and gossiped about us that we were dating. I wished what everyone thought was true.

That's none of your business, bitch!!! Stay away from me, I thought.

I wasn't in a state to respond her. I took large steps that she could be left behind. But she followed me.

'I guess you tried doing the same hanky-panky with her and she too turned you down. You're left thirsty…once again,' she shouted, chuckling and giggling. This boiled my blood. Made me feel like a deep pang in my heart. I felt to hold her from her pony-tail and hit her head on the ground. I turned back and frowned at her.

'Okay, leave. Could you please drop me home?' she added between her chuckles.

'Look, I tell you, stay away from me. Stay the fuck out of my life otherwise I will make you stand here and run my car in your ass,' I screamed out. She was left with her mouth open.

* * *

When I got home, Mom was sitting at the dining table, drinking a mug of tea. Dad was sitting on the couch, surrounded with some files and working on his laptop. He turned to look at me and then turned his focus back on the laptop. I acted to look normal.

Mom put her tea mug on the table and stood up. 'Are you okay? You look disturbed.' She walked up to me. She put her hand on my forehead.

I'm not. Nothing is okay in my life, Mom, I thought.

'No, nothing,' I said. 'I'm just tired.'

'Go, freshen up yourself. I will make coffee for you.'

'No, thanks, Mom. I need to rest,' I said and left for my room.

29.

It had been a week since I approached Niti in library. Since then, I kept struggling to talk to her and she kept ignoring me. She didn't utter even a single word. She didn't even show any kind of aggression. She wasn't interested in showing any kind of human emotion to me. She well showed that my existence doesn't even matter to her. And it was really horrible for me. More horrible than being abused, thrashed and slapped a thousand times. I tried calling her from different numbers as I was blocked, and she hung up as soon as she recognized my voice. I wrote her thousands of apology texts, she replied to none. She even didn't talk with anyone in the class. I scolded myself for making her like that. Wimp thought she wasn't well.

Her silence was killing me every passing day. Her shrunken and expressionless face was choking me inside. And her ignorance wasn't allowing me to breathe. I kept thinking about her all the time. I struggled to sleep every night with a hope that she would talk to me tomorrow, she would abuse me and complain about the mess I had created, and then I would try to explain, would say sorry and would ask her to forget everything and forgive me that we can make a fresh start. And then I would tell her that how much I was in love with her. But nothing was happening. It was turning worse every passing day. And that day, she didn't come to the college. In the evening, as I stared at my room ceiling, a question crossed my mind.

How long shall I keep staring at the things around me and waiting for her to respond to my sorry?

Immediately, I decided that I would go to her place and no matter what, whether I would have to beg her the whole night, I would apologize to her and tell her what I actually felt for her, otherwise my head was going to blow apart as I couldn't stop myself thinking about her even for a second. This mere thought pumped my blood circulation thousand times. I picked up my car's keys and rushed out of my room.

'Vardan, come back on time. You're skipping your dinner these days,' my mother shouted behind as I reached the main door. *I'm skipping life these days, Mom*, I thought. She didn't know I was going to skip breathing if I couldn't see and talk to Niti anymore. I snubbed her concern and came out. I sat in my car and drove off. The whole way up, I thought about the things I wanted to say.

It took me a few minutes of resistance to reach the heavy steel door of her flat. My fingers quivered for a few seconds before pressing the white bell button. Before the door got answered, I looked up and beseeched the God that he could shower me with some magical words and I tell them to Niti that she would agree to listen to me. But nothing came in my mind. It was like the God also wanted to say *fuck off*.

My heartbeats started running faster than Usain Bolt as I heard the gate getting unlocked from inside. She opened half of the door and tried to push it close as soon as she saw my face. I held on the door and pleaded, 'Niti, please. Listen to me. Don't close it. Please.'

She still tried to push the door close and I kept holding it and pleading. I added, 'I will sit here whole fucking night if you don't listen to me.'

She still didn't respond. She wasn't even looking at me.

'Niti, please let me in. Trust me for the last time.'

Trust? At least don't use this word in front of her, my crestfallen heart said this to the wicked mind.

I saw there was a knife in her left hand. I wondered if she would stab me with that knife. We stood quiet for a while. I looked at her and at the knife in her hand relentlessly. She looked down. And then she left the door and walked inside. I stepped in and shut the door. She sat on the sofa and started cutting ladyfingers into a bowl on her lap—I got the purpose of knife in her hand. She wore a black cotton shorts and maroon crop-top. I restricted myself from looking at the bare skin between her crop-top and shorts. I stood there clueless, facing her back. I searched for words and wondered how to begin.

'I know I will play a notorious monster in the book you will ever write on your life. But, what others have done to you? Why are you not talking to anyone in college? You don't even smile these days. Why are you scolding yourself?' I said, standing beside the sofa she was sitting and looking at the centre of her head which seemed to produce volcano soon. She didn't respond. She just increased the speed of chopping. I felt I sounded very stupid. Those were the days everything I did, felt like I was doing stupid.

'She is definitely not going to ask you to put your ass on the couch,' I said to myself. I mooched towards the opposite sofa she was sitting and sat on it. I felt like an uninvited guest there. She was at her best in ignoring my presence there.

I craned my neck forward. 'We...we need to talk, Niti,' I said, fumbling. She kept on chopping. I sat there numb and naive, waiting for her to respond. She didn't. I felt hopeless and prattling before her.

30.

After a few minutes of awkward silence, I abruptly stood up and shouted out, 'Why are you doing this to me, Niti? Why are you not even responding a single word? WHY?' She stopped running the knife in her hand. She looked up and stared at me. I stared back.

'WHY? You're asking *why*?' she yelled, glowering at me. I had already expected her curt responses. Well, finally, she spoke. Last time when I heard her voice was in Chandigarh. I wanted her to keep on talking. It felt some kind of relief to me. It gave me a sense of buoyancy.

I sat beside her on the sofa. I touched her elbow. 'I know what I did was really gross, but...' she cut me off before I could complete. She pushed my hand away. I knew I deserved that.

'I don't want to talk about anything,' she declared. She stood up and marched towards the kitchen. I followed her. She put the vegetable bowl on kitchen slab and stood folding her hands.

'Then, for how long you want me to keep on saying sorry? I can do it for thousand, million or billion of times. Or my whole life if you want me to,' I uttered.

She turned the sink tap on and held on it. I don't know why. Water flew down in full speed. Half of the sink was filled with water. I wondered if she asks me to put my head in that sink to prove I was actually sorry. She didn't. Though, I was ready to do if she would have.

'I have not forgotten anything. And I don't want to be reminded of it again and again,' she yelled, staring in that sink. She turned the tap off. She brought out a tiny water bottle from fridge and guzzled down the whole water in one go. 'I want you to leave me alone, just leave me alone,' she mumbled and came out of kitchen.

'I can't. Even if I want to, I can't stop myself... I just can't live without talking to you,' I mumbled, waddling behind her. She started keeping the sofa cushions in place. I knew she wanted to shove one of those cushions in my mouth that I couldn't speak anymore.

I continued to speak whatever came in my mind. 'Since that day, I have been trying to talk to you every day, but you never cared to answer. You didn't even look at me,' I took a pause. 'You always ignored me. I know there is a storm running inside you. There are millions of bad things you want to say me, but you chose to stay quiet. Even, you're not talking to anyone in college, and that is more painful...to see you like that.' I took a deep breath. I gulped the water gathered near my throat.

'What was left to talk about?' she asked, 'I could never expect what you did-' and she abruptly stopped. She quaffed the pain near her throat. Her eyes turned little soggy, but she tried to remain unaffected. She lifted a blanket lying on the sofa and started folding it. I continued to look at her with an apologetic face expression.

'I know I have let you down. But, believe me, since that day, I have lived every second of my life in guilt. I keep scolding myself every moment. I'm not able to sleep at night. I keep staring at ceiling and the walls of my room, talking to myself. I don't feel like doing anything, go anywhere and talk to anyone. There was only one thing I thought about—*you*. I just longed to talk to you. I desperately wished that you would forgive me and everything would become like before.

But...' I paused to take a breath. 'But I had to go through all this, because, I deserved it. I did.' I felt my eyes had turned little wet. I wanted her to come near me, hold my hands in her and say—everything is okay now, I forgive you, now make a fresh start. But nothing happened like that.

'No, you're not the only one who deserves to go through all that. I also deserve, because, I trusted you,' she shouted. Her words hurt like someone had put a needle deep in my heart. But what she said was the harsh truth. She walked inside the room and started adjusting the bed-sheet. I knew she was doing those avoidable chores so that she didn't have to make eye contact with me.

'Please, don't say like that. You don't deserve it. You don't,' I said. 'Even that wasn't the reason I came to your room that day, reason was something else. I had come to say you something. That wasn't how I actually felt for you; I felt something else, something special.' I wiped a tear drop from the corner of my right eye.

'Yes. You made me feel really special that day,' she murmured. Her sarcastic dig embarrassed me some more. She tried to walk past me. I blocked her way. She looked up and lifted her eyebrows.

'Please. Stay,' I said.

'What?'

'Please. Listen to me. Please.' I had a steady gaze that she seemed to glance away from.

'No point of listening now. Let me go,' she said and tried to move. But I stood blocking her way.

'You remember, I had asked you for fifteen minutes of your life?' I asked. She glared at me. Her face expression told me that she never wanted to hark back to it. Well, I continued, 'I wasted twelve minutes, following my wicked mind. But three minutes are still left. Today, I will follow my heart and use those three minutes to tell you what I actually wanted to confess for a long while.' I paused as my eyes filled with tears. She looked up at me quietly. I took her hands in mine and the very next moment I was on my knees. She didn't react. She didn't act surprised either. Even she didn't extract her hands out of mine.

'This is something I have been trying to tell you since we met. But couldn't. This is something I wanted to tell you on your birthday. But I couldn't. Even I went to Chandigarh to tell you this. But I was stupid. I kept waiting for the right moment. And when finally the moment came, I did a blunder, acting like an asshole. But not today,' I said calmly and paused. A tear drop slipped out of my right eye. She was looking at me. I looked deep into her eyes, her soft hands still in mine.

After fifteen seconds of long stares,

'Niti, I LOVE YOU,' I said. 'I love you a lot. I really do.' I finally did it, with tears in my eyes. She remained silent, looking at me constantly.

I continued, 'A part of me had fallen for you on the very first time I saw you in class. But I didn't know when I fell in love with you completely. It happened gradually—day by day and moment by moment. There are thousands of reasons to love you. I don't know which one to mention first. You're different, completely different than other girls. The way you behave, specially the thing you do for underprivileged children—I love the most. I have witnessed drastic changes in myself after you came in life. I have seen my parents almost failing their love marriage. The reason I hated this word *love*. And I could never imagine that I would ever fall in love. But you completely changed that perception. You made me realize that we can't control when and whom to love. It just happens. And when it happens, life seems meaningless without it. Like it seemed meaningless to me in the last one week.' I stopped to wipe out tears gathered near my eyes. I stood up, still holding her hands in mine. I looked at her eyes, they were almost wet.

'Niti, in last seven days, I just realized that there is not a single second of my life that I want to spend without you. Because I truly love you.

And I strongly believe that you also have a thing for me. I can see that in your eyes,' I said calmly. I prayed to God that she wouldn't break my belief. And I desperately prayed to God that she just says *I love you too* and we hug each other.

31.

'Niti, will you accept my love? Will you be my girlfriend?' I added.

Suddenly, she turned away, extracting her hands out of mine. It scared me like hell. I wondered if she was going to turn down my proposal and break my heart forever. My throat dried.

'Why did you do this, Vardan?' she said, disappointed. I wondered which part she was referring—the part in which I had proposed her or the unexpected things happened in past?

Confused, I eagerly waited for her to speak some more. But, she started sobbing. It increased my anxiety level. I held on her shoulder and turned her towards me.

'Niti, please say it. Please say it if you don't have feelings for me. You have my words I will never bother you again.'

'I knew that you had a thing for me since the day we met. Wimp had told me the very first day you inquired her about me,' she said between her sobs.

I'm going to beat your ass, Wimp, I thought.

Well, she continued, 'And after some time I also started falling for you the same way, because you really gave me some importance, you cared about me and most importantly I liked your company. It made me happy whenever you were around. You were really the first person I felt for someone like that way. And I always wished that you would propose me. I waited. I fucking waited. It was many times that I felt you were going to propose me, but you didn't,' she stopped to clear her throat. Her eyes filled with tears.

'On my birthday, when you stopped and held me in your arms, I thought you were going to say those three magical words. But you didn't... I didn't tell you, but, I was the world's happiest person when I saw you in Chandigarh. I was really happy. I thought I really meant something to you and you could go to any extent to be with me. And when you came to my room and asked for those fifteen minutes I thought finally you were going to say it. But, you...' she stopped as one tear drop fell out of her left eye. She wiped out the tear from her face. She turned other way.

'You're saying it when I have decided that I will never talk to you. I will never...never ever talk to you, Vardan,' she said, almost crying. She sounded the cutest. Finally, she said her heart out. She also had a thing for me. She also loved me. It gave me Goosebumps. All my dead cells got activated and started dancing under my skin. I wanted to smile like never before. But, for a moment, I also wanted to scold myself for not revealing my heart in front of her before.

Your ass gets saved, Wimp, I thought.

I held on her shoulder and she turned to look at me. 'Please, forgive me, Niti. Please, forget everything for the love we have for each other,' I said. We looked into each other's eyes.

'I love you,' I said and hugged her.

'I LOVE YOU TOO,' she finally said it and buried her face in my chest. 'But, I also hate you,' she added, thrashing on my right chest slowly. I felt the sweetest pain. I hugged her tight, kissing on her head. Tears started jumping out of my eyes. We hugged each other for a while. My face filled with tears.

We separated after a long hug. Later, I helped Niti in the kitchen and we had our dinner together. We talked for a while and then I left for home.

* * *

My mother opened the main door. 'Beta, it's too late. Your Dad has just slept,' she said in a low voice as soon as I entered, walking behind me.

'I was late, Mom. But it's fine now,' I said, with extra smile on my face. My *late* was completely different than hers.

She made a confused face. 'Beta, you're acting very strange these days. You hardly talk to me. You keep yourself locking in your room. Yesterday, I saw you talking to yourself. Is everything okay?' she said, deep concerns sketched all over her face. I didn't know what I would have replied to her had she asked me that few hours before. But, now I had a reason to smile and say *everything is okay*.

I moved forward and hugged her. I whispered into her ear, 'I love you, Mom. And everything is more than *okay*.' I grinned looking at her and then I left for my room.

'Take your dinner before you go to bed,' my mother said.

'I already had it, Mom. You go and sleep. Good night,' I shouted.

I jumped on my bed as soon as I shut my room's door and opened my Whatsapp to text her.

`Hey, jst reached`, I texted her, lying on my stomach. I impatiently stared at my mobile screen and waited for her reply. A puckish smile sketched on my face as soon as I saw two blue ticks. I grabbed a pillow and put that under my chest.

Gud. I was abt to ask, she responded with a smiling emoji. Wht are u doin now btw? She wrote one more text before I could reply. Generally, we ask such things when we think what to say next.

Jst lying on my bed and thinking abt u. I mean abt us, I mentioned smiling and wink emojis more than the words in that text. I added, Well thnks for accepting my love.

No, thnks for saying it out finally, she responded with a laughing emoji.

I responded with five different laughing emojis.

She sent me a monkey emoji hiding his eyes with his hands.

I LOVE YOU, I wrote her a text, mentioning a heart emoji.

I LOVE YOU TOO, she wrote back. She too mentioned a heart emoji. I responded her with a kiss emoji.

We kept chatting for some time. And I kept telling her after every second line that how much I was in love with her. And then we talked over the phone before falling asleep.

32.

Last Morning, I was lying on my bed like a soulless creature. I was feeling like I lost Niti and would never get a chance to talk to her. I was thinking like my love for Niti would always be limited to myself only. But today I was with her, in her life, as her lover. Today, I was the happiest person in the world. I felt like the luckiest man in the world—like Neil Armstrong, walking on the moon.

Next morning, I went to Niti's place, picked her up and then we went to college. I had not told anything to Adithya and Sejal till then. I was dying to let them know about the latest news in my life. In my love life. But, I wanted to give them a surprise.

I entered the class with Niti, talking and smiling. Everyone in our class seemed surprised as none of them had seen us talking and smiling in the last few days. But, Wimp and Adithya seemed extra surprised as they stared at us with their mouths open.

We went to Wimp's desk. Niti sat beside her. Wimp stood up and started looking at us one by one.

'Hi, Wimp,' I said, smiling. I gave her a casual hug before she could respond.

'Hi, you're looking very happy today,' Wimp said, sniggering. 'Even you both are...'

Before she could utter anything else, Niti made her ass attached to the desk by pulling her down. Well, I went to my desk, placed my notebooks and sat beside Adithya. He was already smirking, looking at me.

'So?' uttered Adithya, moving his eyeballs.

'So, what?' I asked.

'How did it happen?' asked Adithya.

'Yes, how did it happen?'... 'How did it happen?' Suddenly, we heard two different, but known voices coming from behind. We both turned back and saw Rohit and Mohit craning their neck and trying to shove their head between us. They settled back to their desk hurriedly as we looked at them.

'Why don't you both use a screw driver to remove the unidentified insect in your ass?' uttered Adithya. I laughed. Adithya joined. They both also started chuckling like idiots.

'Let's go outside the class,' said Adithya in between the laughs. He stood up and came out of our desk.

I stopped laughing and said, 'Why???...The professor is just about to come.'

'Fuck everything. I can't wait to hear this,' he murmured and started pulling my hand. 'You told her? You did?' he exclaimed as soon as he dragged me out of the class. His curiosity oozed out from his voice.

'Yes, finally,' I shook my head. And he jumped excitedly to hug me. He seemed happier than me. These are the moments when you realize how much your friends love you.

'When did you do this? What did you say to her? And what did she reply?' he started firing questions at me. 'I want it all. Tell me everything,' he said.

We started walking. We sat on the green ground. He had set his eyes on me without blinking and kept plugging grass out of the ground while I told him how I had proposed Niti last night.

'Why are you telling me this fucking late?' he shouted as soon as I stopped. He threw the dead pile of grass he had plugged out and gathered while I was telling him everything.

'I thought to give you guys a surprise,' I said, removing a grass leaf from my hair.

He dragged his ass on the ground to come closer to me and asked, 'So, what happened after she accepted and said I love you too?' He moved his eyebrows up and down.

'Ummm... we talked for a while. We had our dinner together and later I left for home,' I said, but I knew what he actually wanted to ask.

'Don't tell you both inhaled oxygen together and other bullshit. I'm asking something else,' he mumbled. 'Did you guys make out?' He sounded like he was investigating to get a top secret out of my mouth.

'Don't talk shit,' I gave him a light push. 'We just hugged,' I said. He started giggling, lying on the ground. I smiled seeing him laughing like nuts. Deep inside, I felt jumpy at the thought of making out with Niti, as I didn't want her to remind what had happened in Chandigarh. Not that soon, at least.

'Just a hug? You didn't even kiss her?' he murmured. He plugged out few more grass leaves while waiting for me to answer. He was going to turn that ground into barren land had we sat there for some more time.

'It's not like that...actually I'm not thinking about this getting laid thing this time. I just want her around me. I genuinely love her, man,' I said. I stood up and dusted my ass to clean my denim.

'So, now, you are not rushing to get rid of the virgin tag?' he said, standing up and smiling unnecessarily.

I shook my head.

'I can sense you're genuinely in love this time. Now, you deserve to be loved...to be loved in the form of sex,' he uttered, laughing weirdly and running away from me.

Before I could retort on his *sex eligibility certificate* which he had given me, I saw Niti and Wimp walking towards us.

'You guys are here. We were looking around for you both. Well, why are you bunking the lectures?' Wimp blurted out as they came to us.

'Attending lectures is too boring when we have a reason to celebrate. It's a time to party. Am I right Niti?' said Adithya, smirking and looking at her. Then he winked at me.

'Party is good. But I should also know the reason, no?' replied Niti, smiling.

'Oh, c'mon, it's not a secret anymore,' said Adithya, throwing his hands in air.

'Yes, I also know. I'm happy for them,' shouted Wimp. 'Well, will you guys take me to the party?' she added.

'No. Never,' said Adithya. We all laughed on this, including Wimp.

'Well, does Sejal know about this?' suddenly, Adithya asked. We stopped laughing.

'No, I'm yet to tell her,' I said.

Adithya was ecstatic. He dialled her number and put the phone on speaker.

'Hello,' Sejal answered the call.

'Where are you?'

'In FM class. What happened?' she whispered.

'Which class? Well, we're coming to pick you up. There is a surprise,' shouted Adithya.

'Vardan knows where. Well, I can't join you guys. Will meet you in the evening,' she continued whispering. She had joined a Financial Management coaching in Mukherjee Nagar.

'Fuck your class. We're coming to pick you up,' he said and hung up before she could whisper anymore.

33.

We went to Mukherjee Nagar to pick Sejal up, Wimp with us. Adithya and I entered her class while Niti and Wimp waited outside.

'Are you guys new to the class?' asked the coaching teacher, sounding offended. We didn't care to answer him. We directly went to Sejal.

'What the fuck you both are doing here?' whispered Sejal, rubbing her palm on forehead and looking down. She was already shocked to see us there.

'We came to pick you up. There is a big surprise I'm going to tell you. There is something to celebrate today,' said Adithya, closing the notebook she was scribbling few minutes back.

'You guys are real assholes, I'm telling you both,' mumbled Sejal, glaring at us and packing her bag.

'Hello, sir,' said Adithya, looking at the coaching teacher. Sejal pulled him out of the class.

'You know he is going to screw me up in the next class. You both...'

Sejal stopped as she saw Niti and Wimp. Now, she already had an idea about the surprise we were going to give her. She hugged Niti and Wimp. Then Adithya told her how I proposed to Niti and our story.

'And guess what, they just hugged,' this is how he ended the surprise, leaving me and Niti a little embarrassed.

Well, later, we all went to Hauz Khas Village. We took a table for five in Lords of Drinks Cafe. I and Niti sat holding each other's hand under the table. Sejal and Adithya ordered beer for themselves, and as I, Niti and Wimp weren't in alcohol gang, so we settled with lemonade and soft drinks. We started our small party with Drinks, Paneer Chilli, Chicken lollipop and some other snacks. After a few pints of beer, Adithya started convincing us to take at least one pint of beer. I and Niti completely refused, but he managed to convince Wimp. She agreed to take one pint. And after that she went crazy. Every word we said, she found funny and laughed loudly. And then she lifted another pint and gulped that in one go, like a pro. Adithya cheered for her. Over excited, she pulled us all to the Dj. We all danced, but, unexpectedly, Wimp showed her hidden talent and danced like a mad. Adithya joined her. Meanwhile, I kept gazing at Niti. She looked really happy.

I will always try to make you happy my love, till the last breath I take, I thought while shaking my leg with her and staring into her eyes.

Anyway, it was eleven at night when our party ended. We all came out of the bar, laughing, jumping and hugging each other, like a bunch of happy friends. I offered everyone to drop, but Sejal and Adithya said they would book a cab. Wimp was scared to go home drunk, so Niti suggested her to stay back at her place. Wimp agreed and informed at her home about the same. After cuddling and thanking stuff, Sejal left for her home and Adithya left for hostel. And I drove off towards Niti's home. Niti sat on the front passenger seat and Wimp collapsed on back seat. My whole way up, I played latest love songs, asked Niti to grab the gear stick and placed my hand on hers.

'Love birds,' Wimp mumbled from behind, and that left us smiling

We reached her place.

'Careful,' Niti helped Wimp to get out of the car.

'I'm sorry. I know you guys want to do kiss; hug and other goodbye stuffs...like lovers do. Okay just imagine I'm not here...I should hide somewhere,' fumbled Wimp, murmuring to herself. And then she went to another side of the car and sat down. We literally laughed to see her doing that.

'Beer has worked best on her,' said Niti in between her laughs, 'I hope she falls asleep as soon as we go to the bed,' she added.

'I'm enjoying this side of her. We should also have tried at least one pint,' I laughed, looking at Wimp hiding.

'You don't drink even when your best friends do?' asked Niti.

'Yes. Actually my father drinks a lot. So, my mother has taken a promise from me that I would never drink. She doesn't want me to become like my father,' I said and immediately faked a laugh to make it sound less embarrassing.

She stepped forward and put her arms around my shoulders, 'It's not good to drink. You're a good guy,' she said, her eyes shining with joy.

'This good guy is in love with you,' I said and hugged her. 'I love you.'

'I love you too,' she replied. Everything faded around. The only thing I could see was her pink lips moving slowly when she said that. I felt like placing my lips on hers. I hugged her more tightly and moved my head forward to kiss on her lips.

'Oh, sorry... Sorry, I thought you guys are done,' suddenly, Wimp shouted from the other side of car when my lips were just an inch away from hers. Abruptly, Niti pushed me away. Wimp went back on hiding and sat down again.

'Wimp, I will beat your ass. Come here and go inside with her,' I said, perkily.

'Please don't do that. Don't beat my ass. The only good thing I have,' Wimp said it bluntly, standing up.

Wimp came to us, we hugged each other and I waited until they went inside. Before entering inside, Niti turned back, kissed on her right hand fingers and blew a kiss towards me. I curled up my right hand in air to catch that kiss and placed it on my heart. She smiled and went inside. And I drove towards home, smiling endlessly.

34.

'I feel like holding you like this forever,' I said, sounding orgasmic, embracing her from behind and snaking my hands around her waist. She held on the kitchen slab and moved her neck slowly, her eyes close. My facial skin rubbed against her neck. It seduced me like hell. I got a boner. But, suddenly, she turned to the other side.

'Will you also have some?' she asked, holding a packet of Kellogg's Crunchy Fruit and Nut Museli. She grinned, holding that Museli packet and looking at me impishly, her face expression showed she brought the Museli in between to avoid getting seduced.

'I'm hungry, but not for Museli,' I whispered this cheesy line and pulled her close. I kissed around her neck.

She turned away and grabbed a glass bowl. 'Let me eat then.' She poured Museli in that bowl, put the packet back on the corner of slab and then added some milk in the bowl. She picked a spoon and came out of kitchen, holding that Museli bowl in her left hand. I and my boner followed her to the living room.

We had completed almost one month of our relationship, one month of loving her and being loved, one month of being the happiest person

I had ever been in my life, one month of experiencing the magic love creates, and one month of making each other feel special every day. We tried to spend every minute that life had given us with each other. When we were not together, we talked over the phone and through text. While talking over the phone we almost forget the track of time. Most of the days we talked over the phone whole night that led us to fall asleep in class. We laughed on this later. We visited places together, went for movies and sometimes had a long walk, holding each other's hand. Every passing day I fell for her more and more. After college I went to her place, helped her in cooking, ate dinner with her and we studied together. Sometimes we argued on a topic, where our opinions mismatched. We also had few pillow fights, where I let her win to see smile on her face and ended smiling with her. It had been thousand times we kissed during last one month. We kissed passionately. We kissed at her place, in my car several times, behind the college building, in college parking, we kissed in the corner seat of theatre, and we kissed at my place as I took her there when my parents were not home. We hugged each other as if we were inseparable. Sometimes I lay beside her on bed, we cuddled while lying. There was everything in our relationship a couple has—except one thing. We were yet to take our relationship to the next level. We were yet to make out; we were yet to make love. Every time I held her I felt to make love with her, felt to take our relationship to another level. But there was something holding me back. Deep inside my heart, I knew she wouldn't mind it as she was my girlfriend, drowned deep in love with me. Yet, whenever I tried to make a move I felt nervous, I felt frightened if she gets offended remembering about the last time I had made an unexpected move. But that day I decided to make a move. I decided to go to the maximum extend of love. I decided to make love with her.

After college, we decided to go to her place and study. And I decided to study every inch of her. I smiled inside at the thought of lying naked beside her, after making out. I grabbed her in my arms as soon as we entered and shut the door.

'We shouldn't delay in studying each other,' I whispered in her ear, my chest rubbed against her right arm and chin rested on her shoulder. I felt her warmth; my nose touched her silver earrings. She wore a light pink cotton silk *kurta* and white cotton pants. Her *dupatta* came in between her neck and my lips. I removed the *dupatta* from her neck and kissed there.

She threw her pink tiny bag on the couch. 'Baby, we really need to focus on studies. For last few weeks we have studied almost nothing. You want us to fail in this semester?' she said, calmly. She gave a peck on my lips and pulled herself. 'I'm going to change.' She walked to the bedroom.

Who studies being alone in an apartment with his girlfriend? I wondered.

I walked behind her. 'But we have months for exams,' I said. I placed my hand on the door as she tried to close it.

'And we have a whole life for these things,' she winked at me, closing the door.

Whole life??? She thinks about her whole life with me? Amazing! I thought. I stood there, thinking about my whole life with her while she changed on the other side of the door.

After five minutes,

She opened the door. My mouth fell open and eyes increased its size as soon as I looked at her. She changed into an extra small cherry red shorts which barely covered her upper thighs and a white tank top. I stared at her thighs, shining like white marble. That seemed like a signal for the move I had decided to make.

'You're still standing here,' she said, tying her hair behind. She looked amazingly beautiful.

'I was waiting for you,' I said, stepping forward. I held her from shoulders and glued her back on the door.

'You're looking very hot,' I whispered and moved my head to put my lips on hers. But she kept two of her fingers on my lips.

'I'm looking hot??? Looking???' she raised her one eyebrow.

'No, baby. You always look hot,' I said and lifted her in my arms, her legs wrapped up around my back. I continued and moved towards the bed inside the room. 'You're gorgeous, voluptuous, and the most beautiful girl I have ever seen.' I plonked her on the bed gently.

'You're my miss world,' I said and hopped myself on her. She giggled as if I was tickling in her stomach. For a few seconds, I didn't move and just gazed into her eyes.

'I love you,' I kissed on her forehead.

'I love you too,' she replied with a kiss on my left cheek. First I gave a peck on her lips. Then I placed my lips on hers and started moving them slowly. She responded back. Her lips started moving little by little as mine. And then we started moving our lips quickly as if we wanted to eat each other's lips. We kept kissing for next few minutes. Meanwhile, my right hand invaded into her tank top and started feeling the bare skin of her stomach.

And suddenly, she bit on my lower lip and pushed me away. She stood up and leaped out of the room, laughing. I felt the sweet pain in my lower lip. I ran behind her. She went towards kitchen. I followed her. I put my arms around her as soon as I entered the kitchen. I hugged her from behind, leaving no space for oxygen to pass through.

35.

She sat on the couch in living room, crossed legs, Museli bowl in her lap. The very next moment, I was huddled on the couch beside her. She lifted the spoon towards me, signalling me to open my mouth. Who would like to eat Museli having a storm in their pants? Well, she put the spoon in my mouth as soon as I opened it, ignoring my pang of unwanted food-romance and staring at her fondly. The dull and disappointing truth was the edgy storm in my denim had to take a break until she emptied the bowl in her lap. You just can't ask your girl to leave her food and have sex with you empty stomach—specially, when it's the first time. I watched her feeding herself spoon by spoon. When you're truly in love with someone you find everything sexy they do—even the way they eat.

'I don't think you have any intentions to study today,' she muttered as I gently put my right hand on her bare thighs, arching her eyebrows and smiling wryly at me. She knew my intentions; it was all visible on my face and in my eyes. She might have felt it down when I had hugged her from behind.

'What do you think my intentions are?' I murmured, smirking and chafing her thighs.

'Don't know. Ummm...something...not good for upcoming exams I guess?' she mumbled, running her mouth as she had the last spoon of Museli. She stood up and marched towards the kitchen. I followed her.

She put the empty bowl and spoon inside the sink. I stood behind her.

'Who in the world thinks about exams when they are alone with their hot and sizzling girlfriend?' I muttered, running my fingers behind her neck.

'Wish it were an eligibility to qualify the exams,' she laughed. I laughed back. My boner laughed at me too. It just wanted me to jump on her, like a hungry dog yearning for chicken lying in front of him, completely forgetting my previous attempts and the failures. Well, she lifted an empty water bottle and started filling it from filter.

'Don't worry, we have the whole night to study,' I said, sitting on the kitchen slab. I stared at her cleavage as she lifted both her hands to fill the water bottle.

'Whole night? You don't have to go to home?'

'No. I texted Mom that I and Adithya would be staying at Sejal's place,' I beamed at her.

'You lied to your Mom,' she grinned back at me, taking a sip of water. She left the kitchen, dangling the bottle in her right hand.

'Things we do for love...sometimes to make love,' I said and laughed. I came out of the kitchen, waddling behind her.

'You're a liar. I will tell your Mom when I meet her,' she laughed.

I caught her hand and pulled her towards me. Abruptly, she fell into my arms. Water bottle fell on the ground, leaving a shrill sound—not louder than our heartbeats in that moment. She looked up at me.

'Don't tell her everything,' I whispered, smiling and staring into her eyes. I pulled her close. I could hear her breathe now. I kissed on her forehead and looked at her. She lifted her head up and gave a peck on my lips, her eyes shined with joy. That peck on lips felt like getting a green signal after waiting for a grating one hundred and eighty seconds on a red-light.

I moved my head forward and locked my lips with hers. Our lips met and we started kissing. First I kissed her upper lip slowly and then sucked her lower lip. She responded well this time. That doubled my excitement. I started kissing fast so did she. We started kissing as if we were in a competition to run our lips faster than each other. Our tongue met like two swords. We fell on the couch, kissing each other passionately. Our feet touched the marble floor as only half of our body was on the couch. For next few minutes, we kept sucking each other's lips, my right hand on her neck and left caressing the soft skin of thighs. We slipped down on the floor but that didn't stop us from kissing. We were lost in that kiss for quite some time. Our eyes kept opening and closing periodically. After few minutes of kissing incessantly, we stopped to take some fresh air. I beamed at her, breathing heavily, and she grinned back at me. We sat up against the couch. I sat in front of her and embraced her in my arms. I started kissing all over her face, she sighed when I kissed behind her left ear. My hands crawled up from her waist, head slipping down kissing on her neck. I held her breasts in my hands and shoved my head in between. She breathed heavily when I kissed on her cleavage. I kissed there for a while, almost budging my head in her deep tank top, and then I lifted her top up and shook my head looking at her—to signal her to raise her hands up. After few seconds, grudgingly, she raised her hands up and I removed her top. I held on the couch to keep myself from falling as I almost fainted seeing her in black bra. Half of her breasts peeped out of her bra, which tried to fail my efforts to stay conscious. I regained my consciousness back as she put her hands around her breasts and covered them, smiling embarrassingly. I removed her hands from there and kissed on her half peeping breasts. We slipped on the floor again as I kissed very hard on her half peeping breasts as if I wanted to eat them. I moved my head down, kissing. She moaned and ran her hands into my hair as I put my lips on her belly button.

She pushed my head down and almost pulled my hair as I kissed around her stomach. I kissed there for a while and then sat up on my knees. I held on the elastic belt of her shorts and happened to pull it down, but suddenly she also sat up and held my hands. Astounded, I shook my head looking at her.

'Vardan...no,' she murmured, shrinking her face. My hands froze.

It took me weeks to make this move. Don't ruin it. Not today. Just hug me and make it happen. Just hug me. Damn it! I thought. I implored her, but couldn't move an inch. I was paralyzed thinking it was not going to happen again. I was staring at her mouth, dumbfound, and she was looking down at me, her gaze hooded, shine in her eyes evaporating.

'What happened, baby?' I asked, trying and failing to suppress my rising panic.

'Can we wait for this?' she asked back, putting her right palm on my cheek. 'Till exams...?' I removed my hands from her shorts immediately. I never hated exams in my entire life like I did that day. I was left numb. For next few seconds, I sat there like a zombie.

After sensing an embarrassing silence there, she added, 'Please, don't be angry now.'

I moved close to her, put my palms around her cheeks and whispered, 'It's okay. We will do it when you feel comfortable.' I kissed on her forehead. I said *it's okay*, but it wasn't okay. I wanted to grab her and go ahead. But I didn't.

'You sure, na?'

'Wear your top. Otherwise, I won't be able to wait till exams,' I muttered, faking a laugh.

I was traumatized, saddened and dismayed. But, I tried to act unaffected and normal. I tried to ignore the pang in heart. It had happened with me earlier too—so many times. But, feelings were very different this time. Earlier I used to feel like thrashing them on face, pulling their hair out and not to see them ever again. But this time, I didn't feel like that. I just felt about her comfort, respected her decision. Also, this time I didn't rush to the washroom, I controlled my feelings instead. This time I was in love. This time I was more than a potential boyfriend.

36.

Suddenly, I looked at the door as I heard it open. It was her. She stepped inside. I had come to the bedroom, telling her that I was going to take a nap. She walked and stood beside the bed. She was still in her black bra. I sat up against the bed rest.

'You want to torment me, today?' I inquired, smirking at her. 'Where is your top?' I tried not to look at her uncovered cleavage. Though, my eyes were failing my efforts.

She didn't respond. She moved close and ran her hands in my hair instead, her breasts just few inches away from my eyes. It felt like torture to my eyes. My eyes opened wide as much as I tried to close them.

'What happened to you...? She cut me off by putting a finger on my lips. And then, she lifted my left hand and placed it around her waist and hugged me, my head buried in her chest—lucky nose in the centre. I looked up at her. She was looking down at me, her gaze hooded. She looked gamine and gorgeous. It was enough for a signal. A feeling of happiness ran through my blood. I giggled inside.

I hugged her tight for a while and then yanked her towards me. Abruptly, we fell on the bed. Now she was lying beside me. We glanced at each other and smiled. Every time we looked at each other, we kissed some more. I sat up and flipped her side. Now she was lying on her stomach. I kissed behind her neck and came down kissing. She sighed rapidly. I unhooked her bra, while kissing around her waist. I took down the bra straps from her shoulders and dragged her bra slowly to her stomach. She was still lying on her stomach. I played with my tongue around her bare back. She put her hands on her breasts as I flipped her again. She turned her gaze away, smiling embarrassingly, her eyes close. I got Goosebumps as I gently removed her hands from there. I gaped at her, eyes wide open and hands on my cheeks. I felt plethora of emotions when I put my hands on her breasts. I pressed them gently while kissing all over her neck. She breathed harder than usual. She held my head with full strength as I kissed on her nipples.

Well, suddenly, she sat up and started to unbutton my shirt. Excitement thrilled in every speck of my blood. She lifted her head up to signal me to take my shirt off, and I did it without any delay. Then she pushed me on the bed and sat on top of me. She bent down her head and kissed all over my bare chest, her hair falling all over my face. She went down kissing and tried to unhook my leather belt.

She unbuttoned my denim. 'Remove this,' she whispered and sat aside, pointing at my jeans. I got rid of my denim and removed her shorts. We were only in underwear now. I kissed on her smooth and velvety thighs slowly, bit by bit.

As I was about to remove the last cloth on her body, a part of me just refused to accept that it was going to happen finally. That part of me was shouting inside that something would happen and I would last staying a virgin as usual. That part of me was really afraid. But, that was the day to kill that scared part of me forever.

She folded her knees up to her stomach the moment I tried to remove her black panty. 'No...no...please don't do this, Vardan,' she said, voice as calm as possible. She hid her face behind her palms and smiled embarrassingly. She shied away. I peered into her eyes and I could see that she didn't mean what she had just said. I kissed on her legs and unfolded her knees straight.

I underwent millions of orgasm as I removed the last cloth on her body and saw her completely. That overrode my senses. She moaned heavily as I touched my fingers there. Soft, softest thing I had ever touched. The room echoed with her moans as I kissed there and the inner parts of her thighs. I removed my underwear and lied down beside her. We cuddled tightly. We cuddled naked. Our naked bodies met. I flipped her side and hugged her from behind. She clutched on the bed-spread as my thing touched between her butt-line. Man! I had never experienced this sensation. That turned me crazy. It was one of the best feelings in the world. I was completely out of the world. I breathed desperately and hugged her with full strength as if I wanted our body to dissolve into one entity. She moaned continuously, her nails dug deep into the bed-spread.

My ghosh! If it's feeling this great then how would sex feel? I wondered.

Anyway, after, kissing each other's naked body for quite some time, cuddling tightly, turning and twisting in each other's arms, cherishing the warmth of each other, and sighing heavily, I tried to enter her. But in our first four attempts it didn't happen. In first attempt, it just slipped away. And in last three attempts, she pushed me away.

'This is your first time?' I asked her, speaking calmly. The best thing about our relationship was we had never discussed about our past and previous relationships. I never asked her nor did she.

'Of course,' she said, arching her eyebrows. 'Yours too?'

Technically, yes, I thought.

'Yes, mine also,' I said and smirked.

I tried to enter her one more time. Again, she tried to push me, but I didn't stop this time. First I went slow and gentle. Later, I grabbed her in my arms and increased my speed. Her nails dug deep into my shoulders, but I didn't stop. Finally, I entered her. I just went to another world. The world I didn't want to come back even for a second.

After that I don't remember how long I kept leaning onto her, when she came on top of me and how many times I flipped her on stomach, I just kept climbing her. Our bodies met and we made out. We made love. I got rid of the fucking virgin-tag. Finally. I never knew sex felt this amazing. I always cursed my destiny for not getting successful in doing this so many times. But, now I felt that the wait was worth it. I was happy to do it with her—with the love of my life. Sex feels more amazing when it is done in and with love.

* * *

I opened my eyes. We were lying straight on the bed, next to each other, facing the room ceiling. I turned to look at her. She was already looking at me. We looked at each other and smiled. Her eyes were wet. I put my hand on hers. She clutched it tight.

'Hey, what happened?' I asked her, staring at her.

She shook her head that meant *nothing, nothing happened.*

I turned my side and put my hand around her. 'Did I hurt you?' I asked calmly in her ear.

'No. You didn't,' she replied.

'Did it pain?'

'Initially it did. But then...'

'Then?'

'Then it started feeling good.' She smiled embarrassingly.

'Just good?' I smirked.

'Ummm... first good, then very good and then amazing. It felt amazing,' she stopped. 'I love you,' she ended moving close. She buried her head in my chest. I caressed her hair.

'I love you too,' I said and embraced her.

We kept lying there in each other's arms for half an hour before we made out for the second time. Tired, we sat up and started looking for our clothes.

'Why do we need to wear...when we will have to get rid of them,' I said, smirking, while she gathered our clothes.

She threw my clothes on me. 'Shut up! We won't do it before exams now,' she said, pulling her panty up. She beamed at me, adjusting her bra.

I made a face. 'Two months?' I muttered, putting my legs into the underwear holes. I stood on my knees that my underwear could reach its final destination. I couldn't imagine myself to wait for two months to make out the next time. I could barely wait for next two hours.

Well, that night, nothing was going to stop us from making love. We made out in the kitchen while preparing the dinner. We went on the couch to study and ended making out there. And we made out one more time before we finally decided to sleep at six in the morning.

37.

'Hello,' she answered the call, in a low voice. I had called her multiple times in last one hour before she finally answered.

'Are they still there? And why were you not answering my calls and messages?' Abruptly, I shouted and fell silent, sensing the high tone of my voice. 'Sorry! I was worried about you,' I added.

It was our last semester. Last few semesters we spent loving and caring each other, studying together to clear the exams, leaping with children in NGO's and orphanages, watching repeated episodes of FRIENDS and GAME OF THRONES, visiting places and chilling with our friends, and enjoying sex the best and the maximum we could. We made out almost every next day. We made out in every corner of her house. We made out at Sejal's place, and sometimes at my place when my parents weren't home, of course. We made out in my car twice, and once in a ladies toilet of a mall. Making out in a ladies toilet was really a funny experience that we were not going to forget in our entire life. We often laughed about it. We had also visited Chandigarh twice—I stayed in hotel when she visited her maternal grandparents there. Well, that day we—I, Niti, Adithya, Sejal and Wimp—had plans of movie and hanging out at few places after college. But, she didn't come to college and sent me a text that her father and brother had come to meet her. I was a little surprised as her father had never visited her place during all the time I had known her. Sometimes, she used to talk about her brother, but, she did hardly talk about her father. I knew she didn't like her father much. She used to meet them when she visited her uncle's place, but they had never come to her place. So, I was thinking that what was so urgent that they visited her. I knew he was her father and he could have visited her place whenever he wanted, it was very normal. Yet, I was a bit anxious. I was curious to know *why*. And my anxiety level increased when she didn't respond to my texts which I sent her during lectures. I checked her last seen on Whatsapp—that said *8:49am*, the time she had greeted me good morning. She wasn't even coming online. I called her just after the lectures ended. I turned paranoid when she didn't answer my repeated calls. I just took a long breath when, finally, she answered my call.

'Yes. Just few minutes before...I wasn't with my phone...sorry,' she said over the phone, in slow and rasping voice. I could sense she wasn't doing well. I could recognize it from her voice if anything bothered her

'Everything alright? Why are you sounding very low?' I squeaked. I felt prickling on my scalp. I just wanted her to utter quickly if anything was bothering her.

'Nothing...' she took a pause and spoke after ten seconds. 'Can you come to my place?'

'Yes, I'm coming there. Tell me what happened?' I rushed towards my car.

'Come. I just want to hug you,' she uttered.

I sat in my car and drove off.

What if they found about us and they scolded her? But they would have come to college to beat my ass. No.

What if they want to sell their Janakpuri property where she lived? No, this is nonsense.

What if they want her to get married to the boy of their choice, to get some political gain?

The whole way up, I kept making these useless assumptions about the reason she was sounding upset. The last one increased my heartbeats and made me drive faster than usual.

She hugged me as soon as she answered the door and I stepped in. I put my right hand behind her head.

'I'm here now. Tell me...what's bothering my baby?' I said, calmly, stroking my left hand on her back. I kissed on her head. She didn't respond for next few seconds. She hugged me tight, her head buried in my chest.

Please say something. Tell me, the last assumption I have made is a complete nonsense, I thought.

'Nothing happened, Vardan. Do I need a reason to hug you?' she mumbled under my chest and fell quiet. She looked extra cute.

'Are they getting you married somewhere else?' I couldn't hold it for long and said it out. Her silence was making my assumption stronger.

She looked up at me. 'No! No way. What made you think like that,' she said. I took a sigh of relief.

'Ummm...I saw it happening in a movie last night where female protagonist's father makes her marry to someone else, to get some political gain,' I said. I couldn't hide my happiness and grinned at her. 'They also beat her lover...black and blue,' I added. This brought an impish smile on her face. She thrashed on my left shoulder. Her eyes turned wet while smiling.

I pulled a chair and made her sit. 'Just sit here,' I said. I sat in front of her, my knees on floor and hands on her knees. 'Now, tell me what they said to you that made you upset,' I asked, wiping out a tear gathered near her eyes.

After few minutes of silence,

'They had come to take me...' she said.

'To take you?'

'Yes...to Hisar where my family lives.'

'Oh!...and you didn't go, because, you don't want to stay away from me even for one day... the reason you're upset,' I said and ended laughing, expecting her to join and trying to make the atmosphere a bit funny. But I failed as she didn't join in laughter nor she responded. She stared at me. I shut my mouth and stopped laughing.

'You're not understanding, Vardan. They want me to shift there...permanently. I don't know what's in their mind,' she said. Now it was serious. I felt soreness in my knees. I stood up and sat on the couch there.

'Then what did you say?' I asked.

'First, I told them about college and final exams, etc., but they kept insisting, then I completely refused them.'

'Then?' I asked, craning my neck forward, hands on cheeks.

'Dad left angrily. They didn't even look at me while leaving,' she said and started sobbing. I went to her and hugged her. I rubbed her shoulder, trying to console her.

'What did your brother say?'

'He doesn't have a say in anything,' she paused and continued after a while, 'Vardan, I don't want to go there. I never want to.'

'Don't worry. I'm here with you. Just call me when they come to take you away from me,' I muttered.

She looked up at me. 'Will you fight with them?' she raised her eyebrows.

'No. Never. I will tell them about your wish and rights to decide where to live, what to eat, etc.,' I stopped and tried to control my laughter. But I couldn't. I started laughing. I put my one hand on my mouth.

She gave little punches on my chest. 'You're not being serious. You don't know...there are reasons I don't want to go.' I complained like a little kid. Her cuteness always made me fall for her some more.

'Can we go somewhere? Any peaceful place?' she asked, before I could ask about her reasons.

38.

I parked my car near The Humayun Gate of Old Fort. We got out of the car. We were quiet. I gave her time and space to soothe herself.

'You, okay now?' I asked. We walked towards the fort, leisurely, holding each other's hand.

She nodded.

'Well, what made you that disturbed...the thought of going there with your father?' I asked her. We entered the beautiful fort. One of the best things Mughals left for us.

She looked at me and then looked away.

It's okay if you don't want to tell, I thought of saying it.

'I mean, except the fact that you don't want to go away from me,' I said, smiling. I was the only one who was smiling that day as my attempts to make her smile were failing drastically. 'And I have noticed you never talk about your father. You just skip the topic,' I added. We sat on a rock-box there. It was evening; we could hardly see anyone in the range of our eyes. It was a perfect place to be called as peaceful.

We sat there quietly, that made the place more peaceful.

'It's okay if you don't want to share,' I uttered, sounding disappointed, as I really wanted to know now. I picked a small piece of rock and shot it at an empty Appy Fizz bottle lying at around hundred meters distance. That small piece of rock loaded with my disappointment hit the bottle.

'It's not like that, Vardan,' she paused. She tucked one of the escaped tendrils of her hair behind her ear as it fell on her face. She continued, 'There is something I didn't tell you.' She paused again and looked another way. She took a long breath and continued, 'I didn't tell you how my mother died.' Her eyes filled with tears as she said that. Even my brain got collapsed. I felt like suddenly some moist gathered under my skin, disturbing my blood circulations. I could sense how she would be feeling. Nothing can be worse than losing your mother. I put my hands on hers.

She continued, 'My father told me that she got a cardiac attack.'

'So,' I asked.

'He lied to me. He kept lying to me all his life. She killed herself. My mother killed herself because of him,' she roared. She started weeping. That was the first time I saw her shedding tears like that. I felt a pang in my heart seeing her like that. Also, I was left dumbfound about what she had said.

'You mean suicide,' I asked, hesitantly. Immediately, I felt stupid to ask like that. I scolded myself.

'My father had extra marital affairs. My mother knew about them but she chose to keep quiet. But, one day, she saw him with another woman...in an inappropriate condition,' she paused. She gasped, her face filled with tears. I wanted to hold her in my arms. I wanted to console her that she could stop crying. But I didn't. Sometimes, stopping someone from crying seems like injustice. We should let them cry that the pain gathered near their heart can flow out with tears.

She continued, 'She just couldn't take that and gulped down a full bottle of sleeping pills. She took her life...in the same room I was sleeping.' I was wondering how to respond. My body had turned cold and blood stopped entering the heart as my veins stopped working.

'How do you know about this? As you were just seven when aunty passed away,' I asked. It was a logical thing to ask, but every word I uttered at that time I felt it was illogical.

'Everyone knows. All my relatives know about it. They talk about it. No one tells me directly. But, I have grown up overhearing this shit,' she said, her voice falling weak. I could feel the pain in her voice. She had been enduring it since her childhood. I felt extremely bad for her. Wish I had some super powers that I could bring her mother back to her. My eyes filled with tears, but I didn't allow them to jump out of my eyes. I moved close to her and put my arms around her.

'I wish I were awake that night. May be...I could have done something. I could have stopped her...,' she sobbed under my chest.

'It's not your fault. Even if you were awake, you couldn't have been aware about that. You were just a kid,' I whispered and fell quiet. I wiped out some tear gathered near her eyes.

'This is the reason I never want to go there. It makes me sick when I'm there. That place haunts me about her pain and sufferings,' she mumbled in between her sobs.

'Even I won't let you go there,' I said.

You're stronger than I had ever imagined about you, I thought. I kissed on her forehead.

For quite some time, we sat there quietly, my right hand around her shoulder and her head buried in my chest. I felt wet under my shirt as her tears gathered there.

'You know there is a similarity in between us...I also hate my father,' I broke the silence. I had already told her about my father's drinking habit, his behaviour towards me and my mother, and what he used to become after a few pegs of alcohol.

She sat straight. 'I don't hate my father. I can't even if I want to. I can't undo the fact that he is my father. I have never disrespected him. It's just that I don't want to go to that place and live with him. Vardan, you should talk to your father. Hating someone is never a solution. At least, you should try to make things normal. Talk to him and show him how much you love him. Love can solve everything,' she said. It felt like a setback for me. Well, she relaxed after sometime. We decided to go back home.

We stood up. I put my arms around her waist and stared into her eyes. 'I love you,' I said and hugged her.

'How much?' she asked, looking up at me.

'How much??? Ummm...72.5kg,' I said.

'What???' She made a confused face.

'Yes! Every bit of blood, flesh and bone in my body is in love with you,' I muttered, smiling. She started laughing. I joined her. We laughed together and toddled towards the gate.

'People say one becomes a star after they leave the world. My mother will be one of them. She will be looking at us,' she murmured, walking out of the fort, raising her right hand up and pointing one finger towards the sky. She stared up at the sky without taking a blink as if she was really expecting her mother to appear in one of the stars.

'Will she like me?'

'I guess so. She tried to give me everything I wished for.' We laughed.

39.

'Please, ask your Dad to hire us if we couldn't make it today,' uttered Mohit when Rohit chuckled behind him without reason. One of the two found everything funny whatever the other one of them said, and giggled weirdly.

Anyway, it was just one month to the final semester exams and placements were happening in the campus. Second round of placements were going on that day. Rohit and Mohit couldn't make it in the first round. They must have giggled or chuckled weirdly in the interviews, we wondered.

'Don't worry you will make it. I'm sure,' I said, patting on Mohit's left shoulder. Rohit lifted his shoulder forward. I patted on his shoulder too.

'In case, you guys couldn't, I will definitely talk to uncle about you both. Only last week he was telling me that his company is looking for two good data entry operators for their warehouse,' shouted Adithya, laughing loudly and offering me his hand for a clap. Half-heartedly, I opened my right palm and he slapped on it. Both the losers left sulking.

'You guys are really going to miss them after college,' said Niti, smiling.

'Yeah, these sons of bitches can't be forgotten,' uttered Adithya, throwing a paper-ball at Wimp—standing at a distance. Baffled, Wimp looked at him wrathfully.

'Anyway, you should get ready. You will be facing the panel after thirty minutes. I'm just coming back. I have to meet the coordinator,' he added looking at us. He asked Wimp to accompany him. She said *no*. He held her hand and left, dragging her with him. Adithya got an offer letter in the first round of placements by Capgemini for their Mumbai branch—unfortunately, he was going to leave us in a couple of months. Well, Niti didn't want to leave Delhi—first, she didn't want to go far from me—of course, and the second reason was her NGO stuff. So, she had applied for Google in the second round of placements, as they were hiring for their Gurugram office.

'You're already looking like a corporate employee,' I said, looking at her. She wore a tight grey trouser and white shirt. She stood holding her grey blazer and resume folder in right hand. Her high ponytail wasn't going to let even single tendrils of her hair come out and fall on her face.

She smiled. 'You should have applied and secured at least one offer today. Then maybe you could convince your Dad...and we would be working in the same office,' she said, sliding her hand through her ponytail to bring her hair on shoulder.

'No! Dad will never accept the fact that I would be working for any other company. Even when he is expecting me to join him in business since I completed my schooling,' I stopped to grin and continued, 'He will start forcing me to join him after exams.'

'What will you do then?'

'I want to do an MBA. But, I guess, I will have to accept his offer this time. It can also change the environment at home,' I smirked.

'Yes! Working together will help to reduce the differences between you both,' she said.

'I will figure it out after exams...' I stopped as I saw Wimp running towards us and shouting Niti's name.

'Niti, Niti, Niti...it's your turn,' shouted Wimp, wheezing, her right hand on her chest.

'You scared the shit out of us,' I shouted looking at Wimp. Niti stopped herself from laughing.

'Well, I know you will make it. Yet, best of luck,' I said and gestured to hug her. We hugged comfortably as everyone in our college knew about us till then. She went to the interview room and I waited for her outside.

Smile on her face told that she had made it as she walked out of the room. It was the very first interview of her life and she made it. She seemed really happy. It pleased me.

Well, we celebrated her achievement in college cafeteria and then I went to drop her.

I shut the door close as we entered into her apartment.

'It's time for the final celebration,' I whispered, sounding orgasmic and hugging her from behind as she bent down to put the resume folder on table. Her formal look was arousing me like hell.

'First, let me change, baby,' she mumbled, placing her palm on my right cheek. I grabbed the blazer from her hand and threw that on couch. I turned her side and looked into her eyes.

'I will help you in changing,' I winked at her. I lifted her in my arms before she could respond. I went to the bedroom and plonked her on bed gently. And then I leaned onto her. I started kissing her.

She put her palm on my lips. 'First, shut the door,' she whispered, pointing at room's door.

'You always make me do this as if someone is in the house,' I said, moping and closing the door. I got rid of my shoes and jumped on the bed.

40.

'Do well in your exam, *beta*,' wished my mother as I went to the kitchen and hugged her before leaving my home. It was our last exam that day.

'Mom, I will give you a surprise today,' I said. My mother always asked me sarcastically about the reason of forever smile on my face ever since the day I proposed Niti and she accepted. There were a few times when she caught me talking over the phone late at night. We can't hide things from our mothers for long. She had an idea that I had a girl in my life. It was just that I hadn't told her about Niti directly. So, that day, I had decided to surprise my mother by bringing Niti home after exam and introducing her to my mother.

'What surprise, beta?'

'Just, wait for the evening, Mom,' I said and sprinted out of my house.

I played my favourite tracks while waiting for Niti at Hauz Khas metro station. After ten minutes of waiting, she came and sat in the car, throwing her notes on the dashboard. We hugged and I drove towards college. In our way to college, we rehearsed and discussed about the potential questions which could appear in the exam. She kept going through her notes and asking me few questions to recheck if I was well prepared or not. We reached the college and I parked my car in the parking area.

'Last exam. Last day of college. Going to miss it,' I said as we came out of the car.

She nodded. 'But, we don't have to miss the exam. Walk fast,' she uttered, lumbering.

'We still have twenty minutes and ten seconds left,' I said, clumping behind her. We walked towards the exam hall. She didn't respond.

'You wanted to meet my Mom, *na*??? You're going to meet her, to-day...after exam,' I said, trying to match her speed. She slowed down her speed as she heard that.

'Seriously?' she exclaimed, her eyes shining with joy.

'Yes! We will go to my home. I have told her that I would be giving her a surprise today.'

'But there is an issue,' she said. We stopped near stairs. Our exam hall was on the second floor.

Confused, I asked, 'What issue?'

'Uncle had called when I was in the metro. He told me that Samar *bhaiya* would come to pick me up after exam,' she said. She had told me that she would be staying at her uncle's place after the exams. But she didn't tell me about this immediate shifting.

'He will come here, to college?'

'No...He will come to my place. I also have to do packing,' she said.

'Why didn't you ask your uncle for tomorrow?'

'I did. But, he didn't listen to me. Even I told him that I would come on my own, thinking that you would drop me. But...' I cut her off before she could explain more.

'Okay! We can manage this. First, we will go to my place, I will introduce you to my Mom, and then I will drop you at your place. You can call your Samar *bhaiya* and convince him to come late,' I said all this in just one breath. She smiled, seeing me speak faster than usual.

'Sounds good,' she said. My mobile rang. It was Adithya.

'You go. I'm coming back from washroom,' she said as I took the call. She gestured to walk away.

'Come fast,' I shouted, running upstairs, my left hand covering the phone speaker.

'Where the fuck are you?' shouted Adithya over the phone and disconnected, seeing me stand on the door.

`Where is she?` He sent me a text. He was sitting in the first row and my seat was in the second row.

`She went to the washroom`, I texted back.

Students were settling down. Almost everyone had come except her. Prof. announced to submit our mobiles.

`Baby, come fast. Only five minutes are left. They are snatching our mobiles`, I texted her before submitting my mobile. I switched my mobile off and gave it to the Prof. who was standing on my head. They started distributing the question paper. But she didn't come. I kept staring at the door. And I took a sigh of relief when she finally appeared. She submitted her mobile and went to her desk. Her seat was on the last of last row from right.

41.

Well, answer sheets were distributed and the exam had started. Everyone started scratching their answer sheets faster than one another. I squinted at her a few times during the exam. But she couldn't know it as she was completely focused in writing her exam, without looking here and there. And in last twenty minutes of the exam, I was completely lost in jotting down. I ran my pen faster than in my whole life. I had to stop when the Prof. came and snatched my answer sheet. I looked up, he was glaring at me. I smirked and the Prof. left.

'You took two minutes extra, you rascal,' said Adithya, standing beside my desk. He laughed quietly.

'Couldn't complete the last question,' I murmured, sounding disappointed. However, he laughed loudly this time.

Well, I looked around for Niti. She was not on her desk. No one was in the hall except a few.

She would be waiting outside, I thought. I rushed to the door and peeped outside. I searched around. She wasn't there.

'What happened?' asked Adithya, as I came back to my desk to collect my belongings.

'Niti is not around,' I said and walked towards the Prof.'s desk to take my mobile.

'She writes her exam in the given time. What would she do here?' he giggled. I switched on my mobile and tried her number. Her phone was still switched off. I tried a few times and heard the same *switched off* tone. It made me panic. My face expression changed immediately.

'Don't be paranoid, man! She will be waiting in the cafeteria,' said Adithya. And I rushed towards the cafeteria.

'This is the problem with people like you. First you don't believe in love, and when you finally fall in love, you turn crazy. Can't live without each other for a second,' he added, running behind me. I scanned around as I enter into the cafeteria. She wasn't there. She wasn't in the cafeteria too. Then I saw Wimp, pushing the sandwich in her mouth.

'Where is she?' I asked her as soon as I reached in front of her. She couldn't respond for a few seconds as her mouth was filled with white sandwich.

'Who?' she mouthed.

'Niti... I'm asking about her. Who else in the world I will ask about?' I yelled at her. She stopped eating.

'I don't know about her.'

'You didn't come here with her?' Adithya interrupted.

'No. I came here alone...because I was hungry after the exam,' she elucidated. I and Adithya looked at each other.

'She had left the hall before me,' she added.

'Before you?' asked Adithya.

'Yes! She had left the hall a few minutes before. I saw her leaving,' she said.

'Where can she go?' asked Adithya, looking at me. We gestured to leave. Wimp went back on eating.

'Samar,' I uttered.

'What Samar?' Adithya made a confused face.

'Her cousin brother. He was about to come and pick her today.'

'So, she went with him.'

'But, why didn't she tell me? Why her phone is still switched off? And Samar was supposed to come in the evening,' I murmured to myself. But I was loud enough for him to hear. I tried her number once again. It was still switched off.

'Don't think much. You know she also can't live without talking to you for a minute. There must be a reason that her phone is off. Like, it might have run out of battery or she doesn't use her phone in front of her brother...or like she just forgot to switch it on.'

'Let's go to her place,' I said.

'Maybe, her cousin is there. Don't create a scene. Wait for her to call you,' said Adithya.

'So, I should just keep staring at my mobile till then?' I sounded like I had no life without her. It was true though.

'Calling you is the first thing she will do as soon as she turns her mobile on. So, go home and wait for her call or text,' he said. I nodded and felt like that was the only option I had.

I called her number multiple of times on my way to home and heard the same exasperating tone—*the number you have dialled is currently switched off*. I hit my steering wheel every time I heard this.

* * *

'How was your exam?' asked my mother as I entered.

'Good, Mom! It was good,' I said, calmly. I tried to look tired of exam that she didn't ask me anything else. I put the keys on table and gestured towards my room.

'Where is my surprise?' she asked as I reached my room's door.

'Sorry, Mom. I got late due to exam. Some other day,' I said without looking at her. I felt bad for my mother. I thought I would scold Niti when I would get to talk to her.

42.

I slapped my room's door shut and collapsed on my bed. I called Sejal and told her about Niti's sudden disappearance. She also suggested me to wait. But my heart wasn't ready to wait even for a second. I wriggled to talk to her like a kidney patient wriggles for a donor. I kept calling her number incessantly. And it choked my heart every time I heard that same fucking *switched off* thing. Deep inside my heart I felt like something was wrong. But my mind overruled the feeling of my heart stating that it was due to over thinking. I kept lying on my bed for next one hour, motionless, staring at my mobile screen and desperately wanting to get her call or text. I unlocked my mobile to check the time. It was 4pm. I kept calling her number again and again until I fell asleep.

It was a continuous bang at my door which woke me up. It was Sunita—our new domestic help. I looked at the watch, dangling on the front wall; it was 5:30pm.

'*Bhaiya*! Coffee!' said Sunita as I answered the door. I rubbed my eyes and picked the coffee mug from the tray in her hand. She left. I closed the door and came back to my bed. I put the coffee mug on side table and looked around for my mobile, as I completely came out of my sleep, expecting her call and texts. I bent forward to grab my mobile as it was on the other side of the bed. No call. But, there was a text from her. And that text notification made me nervous and my whole body turned numb. My hand shivered in fear and confusion, heart stopped beating.

That text said; `I HATE YOU, VARDAN`. I tried to re-read that text. I read that more than hundred times in just few seconds. Still, my eyes completely refused to admit what they had just read.

'WHATTTT???' I shouted to myself, mostly in disbelief. I felt impatient and terrified both while opening the full text, thinking what would be inside. Somehow, I unlocked my phone and opened that text. However, it was just a four letter text. Nothing more. I realized her last seen and display picture wasn't visible. I clicked on her profile to check if her status was visible. It wasn't.

'SHE BLOCKED ME???' I murmured to myself. 'BUT WHY? WHY? WHY?' I was totally unable to think of anything at that moment. Something very dramatic and unexpected had happened to my life, but, I didn't know why? I didn't know why the person who loved me in the morning hated me that evening. I didn't know what made her to write that text.

I called her number, desperately wanting to get connected. But, this time, her number was not-reachable. I scolded myself for falling asleep. I walked beside my bed while dialling her number again and again. But it didn't help. It rather blew my head out. Helpless, I called Adithya's number.

'Hey, any news from her?' he answered the call.

'Adithyaaa...she sent me a text. She says she hates me. Bro, she hates me. She fucking hates me. She said that,' I screamed out, rubbing my hand in hair.

'WHATTT??? But, why does she say that? Did you call her?' he asked. That infuriated me even more.

'I don't know anything. Her number is not reachable. I was feeling something must be wrong. She couldn't disappear like that. She could never do that. I don't know why she is doing this,' I almost cried. My throat pained. I felt pang around my nose and jaw line. I felt feeble in my knees.

'Vardan, please calm down for a second. She doesn't hate you. I know how much you guys love each other. Maybe she is furious about something. We need to talk to her. First we need to go to her place. Pick me from hostel gate,' he said. We hung up.

'*Bhaiya*, how was the coffee? I had made it today,' asked Sunita, as I picked the car's key laying on the table.

'It was horrible,' I shouted and gestured to leave.

'Vardan, it's very rude of you,' shouted my mother. I left before she could see my face and know that how rude life was playing with me all of a sudden.

I picked Adithya and we went to Niti's place. In the whole way up, he kept on asking me to calm down and promising me that everything was going to be okay. And I drove, hoping that we could find Niti at her place.

It was locked. Her door was locked when we reached there. My heart and the hope both broke into pieces. I felt very helpless. That locked door felt like someone had choked my throat and I was unable to breathe.

For a moment I just lost my senses and started banging on her door. I shouted her name.

'Vardan, the door is locked,' said Adithya, his hand on my shoulder. I turned to look at him. I wanted to say something. But, I couldn't. I was completely blacked out. I slid down on the door as if there was no life in my body. I sat there frozen for next few minutes until Sejal came. Adithya had called her before I picked him. He told her everything.

She stomped towards me. 'Vardan, it's going to be alright. Just calm down,' she said, calmly and shook me back to life. She repeated it when I didn't move, didn't answer her.

I scowled at her. 'Why are you both telling me the same shit when there is nothing to calm down,' I screamed out. I felt a twinge under my head. I dug my fingers on my forehead, thumbs on cheeks. And the next moment, I broke down. Tears started flowing out of my eyes. They both sat beside me.

'Why is she doing this to me? Why? What made her hate me so much that she doesn't even want to talk to me?' I shrieked while crying. My throat dried. I continued, 'I could sense it when I found she wasn't waiting for me. But, I kept waiting for her call. I didn't look for her. I fucking waited for her call.'

Sejal brought out her phone. 'Wait! I will try to call her,' she mumbled, while calling her number. It was still not-reachable. She checked her on Whatsapp. Even she wasn't able to see her last seen and display picture. Adithya also checked his Whatsapp. He got the same thing.

'She blocked us too,' said Sejal, slapping her phone on her right thigh. 'Try to connect her on Facebook or Instagram,' she added, looking at Adithya. And they both started looking for her on Facebook and Intagram. But, they couldn't.

'Man! Fuckkkk! She hasn't blocked us from anywhere. She just deactivated all her accounts,' uttered Adithya, running his hand into his hair and taking a long breathe. Sejal nudged him to stop. This frightened me even more.

'Guys! We need to figure out how to contact Niti. Let's go to my place first,' said Sejal, standing up and pulling me up to make me stand. I removed my arm out of her grip.

'No! You both go. I won't go anywhere. I will sit here and wait for her. She can't do this to me. She will come and talk to me. She will have to tell me what is making her to do this,' I declared, sounding painful and thwarted.

For next two hours, they both kept insisting me to go to Sejal's place. They tried to convince me that everything was going to be alright. But I didn't move an inch. I sat there motionless. My whole body started shivering in fear. I felt like I just lost her.

And, all of a sudden, I started shouting, my eyes wet. 'It's been more than eight hours that I last spoke to her. We didn't live without talking with each other for this long. The very first thing she did when she woke up was to call me and talk to me. She became angry if I didn't give her any call or text for two three hours. If she is at her uncle's place and anyone is around, she comes out of the house or even goes to toilet to talk to me. But, what happened to her now? Why is she not talking to me? What in the world can make her hate me? Does she really hate me? But why? Why? Why? Why would she?' I stood up and continued shouting loudly, 'SHE NEEDS TO TELL ME WHY... SHE FUCKING NEEDS TO TELL ME.' It was so loud that few people from nearby buildings peeped out of their windows and balconies.

Sejal came near and put her hand on my shoulder. 'Vardan, let's go to my place. Maybe she went to her uncle's place. Don't create a scene here,' she whispered. I had no energy even to resist now. I walked behind as they pulled me.

I sat on the back seat of my car like a soulless creature. I was unable to put my hands on steering and focus. Sejal drove off.

43.

'Vardan, you need to speak,' said Sejal. I was quiet since we reached her place. I sat on the floor, against the couch in living room. They both sat beside me.

'Tell us if there was any fight or argument between you both?' she asked this question for the third time.

'No! We didn't fight. There was nothing wrong in between us. There was just a small argument between us that was around eight weeks ago,' I replied. I wish there were a fight in between us so that I could have a reason for what she was doing. There was none.

'Then why would she do such strange things...? Deleting all her accounts...saying she hates you...there must be a reason...a big one,' she murmured. She was loud enough that we could hear.

'Did she ask something during the exam and you ignored her?' asked Adithya. Sejal frowned at him for asking such intelligent question.

'What did you guys talk before she went to the washroom?' asked Sejal. She wasn't ready to give up. She tried her best to find a reason.

Deep inside my heart I felt like there was nothing in the world that could make her act like that.

'I told her that I would introduce her to my mother in the evening,' I said.

'That's the reason. She didn't want to take the relation to next level. And she just couldn't say it,' uttered Adithya.

'What are you talking about...She is a girl with some values. Relationship and commitments really matter to her. Even if what you are saying is true then why would she say that she hates him? Why would she disappear?' shouted Sejal.

'I even can't imagine this. I have been there with them most of the times. I have felt their love. I always felt they can do anything for each other. But then, girls are unpredictable. Khushi also behaves very strange sometimes,' Adithya shouted back.

'Are we talking about your girlfriend here? Can't you please stop scattering your shit here? Nonsense!' yelled Sejal. I wanted to say that please don't fight because of me. But I couldn't.

'Then you tell us that why Niti is doing this to him? He loved her like anything. And what is she doing? She disappeared all of a sudden... without even giving a reason,' Adithya yelled back. He was taking my side. But what he said hurt me a little more.

Someone rang the doorbell before Sejal could yell at him. We all looked at the door. I wished it was Niti at the door. I wished her to come to me running and hugged me as soon as the door got answered. Sejal went to answer the door. I kept staring at the door without taking a blink until it got answered. It was her cook aunty. My hopes and wishes got cooked. Cook aunty went to kitchen to prepare the dinner and Sejal closed the door.

'Why don't we try contacting her cousin Samar?' exclaimed Adithya as Sejal came and sat beside him. I got a ray of hope as he said that.

'Yes! The only way to contact her for now. She must be at her uncle's place,' she said and stopped to look at me. 'Vardan, do you have his number?' she added.

Fuck! I don't have his number. Nor I know his exact address, I thought, scolding myself.

'No! I dont. I have met him just once,' I mumbled.

'We can contact him through Facebook. Hope he too didn't block us,' uttered Adithya. He really started giving some useful suggestions. I was friends with Samar on facebook. So, we started searching him on Facebook. In next one hour, we went through hundreds of profiles with the name Samar, but, we couldn't find him. Then we went through my mutual friends and People may you know list. One profile matched with his face but the name was Samrat. That confused us, so we went through that profile carefully. However, I could recognize his face, but, finally, we got a picture of him with Niti. It was an old picture where Niti was in school dress. I gazed at that picture for a few minutes. She looked really cute in that. And I came back to life as Adithya cheered.

'Yes! Yes! Yes!' he shouted out in excitement. That felt like a little victory. My eyes filled with hope and tears. I tried to hide my tears.

I wrote him a text and sent. `Hey! Samar. Please get back to me as soon as possible. It's urgent!` And we waited for his reply.

After forty-five minutes,

'Why is he not responding?' uttered Adithya. So, I wasn't the only one who was desperately waiting for his reply.

'Seems like he isn't that active here. We need to wait,' responded Sejal, sounding the most optimistic there.

'Didi! The dinner is ready! I have cleaned the kitchen too. I'm going now,' shouted the cook aunty and left.

Now they both started insisting me to eat. But I refused. Then they started threatening me that they would also not eat anything if I didn't. Unwillingly, I had to eat one *chapati*.

After dinner, we kept waiting for his reply until we fell asleep. I slept on the couch there.

* * *

Next morning.

I saw Adithya was lying on the floor as I woke up. Sejal was awake and walking around, brushing her teeth. I rubbed my eyes and opened my inbox to check if Samar had responded to my text or not. I fell disappointed as he hadn't even seen that text.

'What happened? No reply?' Sejal mouthed, running toothbrush on her teeth.

'He hasn't come online yet,' I responded.

'He will. We need to wait,' she said. 'Vardan, you should go home. Aunty must be worrying about you.'

I nodded, looking at Adithya.

'Don't worry about him. He will go on his own.'

'Thanks!' I hugged her and left.

* * *

'Where were you last night?' screamed my father as I stepped inside my home.

That day I wasn't even able to respond him curtly. I walked inside, snubbing his unwanted concern.

'Look at your upbringing. Look at his attitude. He doesn't care to respond to his father,' he shouted at my mother. I scolded myself for disappointing the two lady loves of my life. One hated me for some unknown reasons and the other one was being yelled at because of me.

'Where were you, beta?' asked my mother.

'I was at Sejal's place,' I said, calmly.

'College is over now. Do party, throw away my money for next two or three days more. Then you will be joining the company. I don't want any excuses this time,' he shouted.

I wish he knew what I was going through. I wish he put his arms around my shoulder and would say—*it's going to be alright beta. This is bad time! It will be over*!

Anyway, I didn't respond to anything. I went to my room and slapped the door hard to shut it, as hard as life had slapped me.

44.

'You're the same guy...we met at the police station?' asked Samar, pondering and pointing a finger at me. He responded to my text after three days. I convinced him to meet, telling it was really urgent. I didn't mention anything about Niti. He agreed to meet me at a cafe in Cyber City, Gurugram. He came there with his fiancé Ananya. I went there with Adithya and Sejal. And yes, still, there was no news about Niti. Those three days without her passed like thirty years. Every second I yearned to talk to her, to see her and to get her back in life. I didn't know when that longing was going to end. Seeing Samar felt like it would end that day. I reached there at 11am.

I extended my hand to greet him. 'Yes! We met at the police station. I'm Niti's friend.' We shook hands. We all shook hands with each other and sat.

'So, tell me what the urgency was? Why did you want to meet me?' asked Samar, sounding as if he was in hurry and removing his sunglasses. Even I didn't want to delay. I desperately wanted to hear from his mouth where she was and if she was okay.

'Actually, there is no news about Niti for last three days.

Her number is not-reachable. She is supposed to be at your place. She told me that morning. You were about to come to pick her up. How is she?' I asked.

He looked at Ananya and remained quiet. I, Adithya and Sejal looked at him for an immediate answer.

After a few minutes, he spoke. 'I don't know anything about her. I'm also trying her number.' And he broke all our hopes. It felt like someone hit on my head with an iron rod. My head got blocked in that moment.

'What the fuck!' shouted Adithya, sounding disappointed. Samar glared at him. Adithya glared back. Sejal asked Samar twice. But he gave the same answer. None of us believed what he had said. It felt like he was hiding something. It was all on his face. He looked away.

And suddenly, he stood up. His fiancé followed him. They gestured to leave. Abruptly, I stood in front of him and started pleading.

'Please tell me if you know anything about her. I really love her. She disappeared suddenly. I don't even know the reason. I'm really worried if she is well or not. I can't sleep at night. I'm unable to breathe properly without her. Please tell me,' I almost begged him. I was about to cry.

'They really love each other. Please tell it for the sake of love,' said Sejal.

'Yes! They do,' added Adithya as Samar looked at us.

Ananya whispered something to Samar. It felt like she was asking him to open his mouth.

'Look, she swore me not to disclose this to anyone. But, I'm telling you because she feels you really love her,' he began speaking, pointing at Ananya, and stopped.

Go ahead! Say it fast! I thought.

He continued, 'That day, her number was running switched off when I called her at around 3pm. So, I went to her apartment. She was there, packing her bags. I thought she was preparing because she had to come to my place. But, unexpectedly, she refused to come with me. I noticed there were tears in her eyes which she was trying to hide. I asked her about the reason, but, she didn't tell me. Then she said that she wanted to go very far from all this. She didn't even want to live in the surroundings of this city. I insisted her to tell me about the reason she was upset. But, it was of no use. She had been a stubborn since starting. I knew she wasn't going to tell me anything. Then I insisted her to come with me. But, she didn't agree. Then she took a promise from me that I would never share this with anyone and said that she would call me. She also said that she would come to meet me when she would feel good. Then I came back to home. And later when I dialled her number, it was not-reachable. Nor did she call me.'

What he had just said really infuriated me. I also scolded myself for not going to her place after college. She was there. I got frustrated.

'YOU STUPID BAG OF STEROID! You let her go even when you noticed her crying,' I screamed out, pushing him away all of a sudden. 'What kind of a brother you are?'

Abruptly, he hopped on me and caught me from my shirt collar. He held my neck as if he wanted to use all his gym work outs on me that day. His thumb nail dug into my neck. My neck was choked. I felt difficulty in breathing. His hand was very hard and heavy.

'I'm her brother that's why I tried to respect her decision. None of us ever tried to control her. She has gone disappeared because you must have done something to her. I will kill you if anything happens to her,' he screeched, holding my neck in his hand. Everyone tried to separate both of us, but he wasn't ready to lose his grip. I wanted to say something, but, I couldn't utter a word. I felt I was going to die that day.

And then, Adithya bit on his hand. He ran away and stood at a distance, securing me out of Samar's grip. Adithya had really put his life at risk for me that day.

Samar screamed in pain, gesturing to run behind Adithya, but Ananya caught him.

'Have you gone crazy? You want to kill him?' Ananya shouted at Samar. 'You almost choked his neck.' She glared at him.

'Why the fuck he pushes me? And I'm a bag of steroid?' he complained, rubbing his hand where Adithya had bit him.

'I'm sorry for my behaviour. I hope you guys can understand what I'm going through. I have no news about the person I love the most. She went disappeared without even telling me. I had lots of expectations from you...but,' Ananya cut me off before I could complete.

'See, we understand your situation. We will definitely let you know if we get any news about her,' she said.

'And guys! Sorry on behalf of Adithya. He just couldn't see him dying,' interrupted Sejal. Ananya and Samar left.

Adithya came to me running as Samar left. 'Are you okay?' he asked, observing me neck.

'He got scratches. This one is deep,' said Sejal, showing my scratches to Adithya. I got scratches all around my neck. Two buttons of my shirt were broken. Blood was flowing out of the scratch which I got from his thumb nail. But I didn't feel pain of these scratches. Because, these scratches were too small than the scratches in my heart. Scratches on my neck could be healed in a few days, but, I didn't know when the scratches on my heart were going to be healed.

45.

'I want to beat that Motherfucker's ass! Fucking liar!' Adithya blurted out, as we walked to leave. Sejal adjusted my shirt. They both seemed more in pain than me. I didn't know I had to feel blessed to have such true friends like them or to keep continue feeling terrible about Niti's disappearance.

'Put some here,' Adithya said to Sejal, stroking his finger on a scratch below my left ear. We were at Sejal's place and they were putting balm on my visible scratches. I wish there were any balm to put on the scratches inside my heart. I sat on the couch as quiet as departed, thinking where Niti would be if she wasn't at Samar's place.

'Bring some water for him,' Sejal said to Adithya. He stood up and rushed to the kitchen. He came back with a water bottle in his right hand and two Heineken beer pints dangling in left. I gulped some water and they started gulping the beer.

'He was good before falling in love. At least, he was happy all the time,' Adithya blurted out, after finishing half of his beer.

'I don't think it's a good time to discuss this.' She tried to stop him. But the beer in his stomach didn't allow him to stop.

'Hmmm...Good time! Yes! It's not a good time. I can't see him like this. Can you please tell me that when will we get that Vardan back who was always ready to chill out? Who used to make fun of me and laugh weirdly...Good time...' he shouted, grinning bizarrely.

'Adithya, stop it. And don't drink if you can't hold it,' yelled Sejal, taking the pint from his hand. I wanted to interrupt and stop them from fighting. But, I couldn't.

Abruptly, Adithya snatched his beer pint back from her hand and shouted, 'You had to stop it. You asked him to become a potential boyfriend. He tried and fell in love. Now see what he is getting. She hates him. But why? What did he do?' He gulped the remaining beer in bottle and stoop up to fetch one more for himself. I wanted to stop him from accusing Sejal for everything. I wanted to say him that falling in love with Niti was the best thing I did in my life. But I couldn't. I was just huddled on the couch, torpid.

'Bring one more,' I said.

'One more? For her? She takes time to go for the second,' he muttered and gestured to walk.

'Bring one more for me. I want to try it today. Maybe it can help me not thinking about her...at least for some time,' I said. He stopped and looked at me, astonishingly.

'Yes! It helps...but,' Sejal cut him off before he could complete.

'Are you out of your mind?' asked Sejal looking at him. He shook his head. Then she looked at me. 'Vardan, don't. You shouldn't if you don't.'

'It's okay! It won't kill me,' I said, calmly, fixing my eyes on Sejal. Nothing can kill an already dead person. Anyway, I looked at Adithya. He went to kitchen and came back with two pints. And this is how I started drinking. First, I took one sip. It tasted like hell. And then I gulped the whole pint of beer in one go. Sejal tried to stop me, but she couldn't. I stood up and marched to kitchen to get another one for me. I wasn't drinking because I wanted to try it. I wasn't drinking to have fun and chill out, but in a try to stop thinking about her.

'Okay! You're drinking it! But, go slowly. Gulp it sip by sip, No one is snatching it from you,' said Sejal, as she took last sip of her first pint.

'Yes! We're not snatching. It's all yours!' he said, hoisting his beer up. He put the bottle on floor as we didn't lift our bottle to hoist with his.

For next few moments, we gulped the beer in silence. The taste started feeling normal. But it had started hitting my head. I also felt like vomiting. However, it didn't help. I couldn't stop thinking about her.

'Yes! Her grandparents,' suddenly, I started murmuring to myself, loud enough for them to hear.

'What?' asked Sejal.

'I'm going to Chandigarh. She will be at her maternal grandparents. I'm sure,' I uttered, standing up.

'Today? We're drunk. We can go tomorrow,' mumbled Adithya, lying against the couch.

'WE DONT HAVE TIME. I CANNOT WAIT,' I screamed loudly. 'Last time I waited and see what happened. Didn't you hear what Samar said? She was at her apartment when I was waiting for her call.'

'I'm coming with you,' said Sejal, standing up.

'I will also come,' uttered Adithya, trying to stand up.

'No! You will stay here. You aren't able to stand on your own,' declared Sejal.

* * *

'Two tickets for the next flight to Chandigarh,' said Sejal. We were at the New Delhi airport. Our flight was at 6:15pm. We waited in the gatehouse before boarding. My eyes were closing because of beer. But I forced them not even to blink. I was becoming impatient. I wanted to knock her grandparents' door as soon as possible. I was being very sure that we would find Niti there. I had gut feelings about it.

It was 9pm when we reached her grandparents' house. My hand shivered when I rang the doorbell. I wished Niti answered the door. But she didn't. Her grandmother answered the door instead. We asked her about Niti.

'No! Niti didn't come here. Even she didn't call us for last few days. What happened? Is everything alright?' this is what her grandmother said. It shocked me. I took two steps back. My gut feeling had failed drastically. I started feeling dizzy. I wasn't prepared for what her grandmother had just said. The last thing I heard was Sejal screaming out my name before I fainted there.

46.

Sixty days, that's how long it had been. Since I fainted in Chandigarh and Sejal and Niti's grandparents saved my life. Still, there was no news about her. Still, I was trying to figure out the reason she went out of my life. Still, I was wondering why she hated me. I went to Hisar, where her father and brother lived. But, they didn't have any idea about her. And they didn't seem to care about it.

Well, Sejal and Adithya were with me most of the time those days. That day they were at my place.

Adithya received a message and made grumpy faces while reading it to himself.

'What happened? Why are you making crabby faces?' asked Sejal, pinching him in his legs. We were in bed in my room. I sat against the bed rest, reading Niti's old messages. There were few messages where we vowed each other that we would always live together. Well, Sejal sat beside me and Adithya sat in front of her, cross-legged.

'Got a text from Capegemini,' he said.

'Then?'

'Have to submit my documents, following a link they have sent. Next week joining,' he muttered. He had hung his head down.

'Then why are you making crabby faces? Well, we should congratulate you or should feel bad that you will be leaving us in a few days,' she smirked.

'You should do nothing as I'm not going,' he said. Abruptly, I kept my phone aside and turned to look at him.

'Not going? But why? This is the best offer to start your career,' she shouted. 'Khushi doesn't want you to go?' she completed in one breath.

'No, she is very happy about it. She even says she will shift to Mumbai with me,'

'Then? What is stopping you,' she stopped and looked at him for an answer. Then she turned to look at me. 'Vardan, ask this asshole? Why is he talking nonsense?' she said. She seemed really concerned about him. So did I.

'What happened to you? You got a good package. Your girlfriend is happy about it. Everything is going good. Then why do you want to fuck it?' I asked, calmly.

'No! Everything isn't going good. I cannot go leaving you like this. I cannot go that far to make my career bright knowing that my best friend is going through hell. I cannot,' he said, shaking his head.

No Man! Please don't fuck your career because of me, I thought. It was emotionally draining to hear that. On the other hand, God didn't fail me at friendship, at least.

I dragged myself close to him and put my left hand on his shoulder.

'Bro! I'm good. Trust me. And don't worry. Sejal is here. We will come to Mumbai to meet you,' I said, right hand palm on my chest, gazing into his eyes. Sejal nodded in my support.

He removed my hand. 'You're good? Just look at yourself bro! You didn't even shave for last two months. You look fragile under your clothes. You eat your food just because you don't want aunty to know about the mess in your life. You keep drinking just to stop thinking about her. You keep talking to yourself relentlessly, asking for the reason why she went away. And you say everything is good?' he yelled at me in one breath. His eyes turned soggy. It brought tears in my eyes. I looked at Sejal. Her eyes were also filled with tears.

I wondered what to say. And he continued before I could say something.

'I will go to anywhere in the world. But, only after, things turn normal. After you find Niti back. Till then, I will be with you. No matter what! And no one will force me now,' he declared, sobbing. Between all this, he made my hope of finding Niti back stronger.

Tears started rolling out of my eyes. I felt pang from jaw to my throat. I moved forward and hugged him.

'Didn't I always tell you South Indian people are very emotional,' uttered Sejal, smirking, sobbing and pointing at Adithya. He really made us love South Indian people.

'See, you made the toughest girl in the world cry,' I mumbled, laughing in between my sobs. Sejal also joined us. We hugged together.

'Sorry for calling you asshole all the time,' Sejal said to Adithya. We separated and sat back.

'See guys! I'm very talented. I can find a job for myself in Gurugram or Noida. I don't need to go that far for a fucking job,' he said and ended laughing. Unwillingly, I joined him in laughter.

No luxury in the world can replace true friends. Sometimes, I wonder how it would have been without Adithya and Sejal in that worst phase of my life.

* * *

I wasn't very active on Facebook. I hardly posted stuff there. My last post was three years ago, a picture of me, posing with my car. But that evening I drank a lot and made a series of posts on Facebook.

Post one, at 7:47pm:

I'm blessed to have you both. #Bestfriendsforlife. I tagged Adithya and Sejal in that post.

Post two, at 8:05pm:

We promised each other that we will always live together. Then why did you do this to me? Why? What had I done? Didn't I love you more than anything in the world?

Post three, at 8:38pm:

Baby! Please come back, na. Please come back. I cannot live without you. I miss you a lot. I won't say a word. I won't scold you for anything. I just want you. Please come! Please come!

Post four, at 9pm:

I Know You Love Me Too! You Do!
I always wanted you! You had that clue!

I went slow! This time I didn't want to blow!
It started with friendship! A door to our relationship!

You smiled, your eyes were blue. Whenever I saw you, I fell more for you!
I was waiting for the right moment to tell you! But you always knew how much I loved you!

Right moment came, I didn't tell. Whatever was in my heart, I couldn't spell.
I made a wrong move. Everything turned in the groove.

I broke your trust! You covered your heart with a crust!

I was scared! Yet I dared!
I pulled you in my arm! You smiled, eyes filled with charm!
I said I love you! You said it too!

Together we slept! Our heart crept!
Why do you hate? It cannot be our fate! Baby, please come! I cannot wait!

I miss the glances we stole in the class. Now I glance at the beer glass.
I miss our pillow fights. My heart screams for its rights.
I Miss how we cuddled. Come, see, how I'm fuddled.
I miss how I played with your hair. Now, I have no one to glare.
I miss how you always kissed on my head. I couldn't know when I turned that bad!

You miss me? I do!
I Know You Love Me Too! You Do!
I Know You Love Me Too! You Do!

47.

Whenever I put more beer in my liver than usual I slept at Sejal or Adithya's place. But that day I went home. It was 11:30pm. My mother answered the door.

'It's late,' she said. She stared at me as I was unable to stand properly. I held on the door to keep myself from falling.

'Did you drink, beta?' she whispered, astonishingly. She covered her nose with her palm. I was stinking of alcohol.

'Mom...I...' I mumbled and looked away.

'Go to your room. Your father is sleeping,' she whispered. I glanced at her. She looked really disappointed. I tottered towards my room. I fell on my bed and lay against my back, legs dangling down to the bed.

After ten minutes,

My room's door fell half open. It was her, my mother. I sat up quickly. She stepped in. I hung my head down in shame. I remembered about the promise I had made to her. I broke it. I had been breaking it for last two months. I wondered if she also started hating me like Niti. But here, I knew the reason. I was already feeling guilty about that. She walked towards me. I felt she would burst out at me. I covered my mouth with palm as she stood beside me.

She put her hand on my head. 'Vardan, what happened, *beta*? I know there is something you're trying to hide,' she asked calmly. I wasn't expecting that sweet gesture. She continued when I didn't respond for next few minutes. 'There is something that is bothering you inside. You can tell me. I'm your mother.'

Abruptly, tears gathered near my eyes. I tried very hard to keep them from coming out of my eyes, but I failed. Tears started flowing out of my eyes. May be it's because the unexpected gesture from my mother or the feeling of guilt for breaking the promise or the pain and frustration I had been enduring for last few weeks or because of all of these reasons, I couldn't stop myself from breaking down. I started bawling in front of my mother. Tears gathered near my chin.

'WHAT HAPPENED, *BETA*?' surprised, she asked. She sat beside me, wiping out my tears from her *dupatta*.

'Mom...I'm sorry,' I uttered between sobs.

'It's okay, beta. I'm not angry at you.'

'Mom, I love you! Please don't hate me. Please don't hate me,' I mouthed in guilt.

'Why are you saying this, Vardan? I can never hate you. You're my son. I have always been proud of you,' she said, hugging me. I buried my head in her chest. 'Which mother in the world can hate their child?' she murmured to herself. She rubbed her hand on my back and tried to console me. It gave me some relief. I stopped sobbing.

She made me sit straight. 'Now tell me what is bothering you? Is it something about any girl? You love someone?'

She repeated her question when I didn't answer for a few seconds.

Then I finally told her about Niti. I told her everything. I also told her that how Adithya and Sejal had stood beside me during all that.

She was also confused about Niti's unexpected move. She also suggested me to wait for her. 'She would come to you if she really loved you,' she said. But, now, my mother was more worried about me.

She lifted my right hand and put that on her head. Her eyes turned wet. 'Beta, promise me you will never hurt yourself. Otherwise, I...' I cut her off before she could complete.

'Mom, I won't do anything else to disappoint you,' I promised.

'Also, don't drink,' she said. 'Don't drink too much if you do,' she added. She smiled. I hugged her.

48.

One And A Half Year Later

'Did your boss suck your ass today?' I uttered, pulling my seat belt. That was a Saturday evening and I had picked Adithya from his office in Golf Course Road, Gurugram as we used to go to a beer cafe in Hauz Khas every weekend. It had been around one year that he had joined the job. That day he was very quiet since he put his ass inside the car. He looked disturbed. I thought he might have a bad day at office.

Sometimes, I couldn't believe it had been eighteen months breathing without her. Sometimes, it felt like yesterday. But I didn't lose the hope. I still believed she would come back to me. But Adithya and Sejal had started suggesting me to get a new girl and move on. They didn't want me to keep suffering. My father asked me to join his company almost every day. I just snubbed him. I was still not prepared mentally. And my mother bothered thinking I would marry or not now if Niti doesn't come back.

Anyway, Adithya didn't respond to my concern. He opened the glove box and lifted out a beer cane. He started gulping beer. I drove in silence till we crossed the Gurugram toll.

'Will you say something?' I asked, taking the beer cane from his hand.

He shook his head up. I took a sip of beer and gave him the cane back.

'Tell me what happened? Did your boss say something?'

'No! It's Khushi,' he said, making quirky faces. He looked out of the window.

'What did she do?'

'She said she wants to breakup with me.'

'WHAT??? Why?' I was shocked.

'She thinks I don't give her time. We had a little argument on this. Now she isn't taking my calls,' he revealed, with his head hung down, and ran his hands inside his hair.

'AT LEAST, YOU KNOW THE REASON,' I murmured and fell quiet. I focused back on driving, thinking about Niti.

'I'm sorry. I didn't mean to remind you of Niti,' he said. Immediately, I felt I acted like a selfish.

'No! Even I should say sorry. I ignored your concern,' I repented.

'Leave all this. Tell me why Sejal did not come?'

'She said one of her relatives is visiting her today,' I said. We reached our destination.

We sat on a couch there and ordered beer and snacks. He went to the DJ after gulping some beer and started dancing as if he had touched any naked electric wire. I saw him from the couch, taking small sips of beer. And then I noticed, on my right, there was a girl. She was in a black one piece which ended till her mid thighs. She was standing near the bar and constantly staring at me. I looked away and tried to ignore her. I started sipping up my beer and enjoying Adithya's mad dance. Then I squinted at her. She was still staring at me.

Adithya walked to me, dancing. He bent down to say something. 'I guess, she is hitting on you,' he shouted in my ear because of the loud music there.

'Bro! You dance like...like no one can do. You go and dance! I'm watching you,' I shouted back instead, lifting my beer mug.

'Bro! Look at her. She is hot. She looks like a medicine to all kind of pain,' he exclaimed.

I gave him a little push to register my snub. But, the alcohol running in blood refused to stop. We walked towards that, whispered something to her and went back to DJ.

And the next moment she started coming towards me, walking like on a ramp. I hung my head down, peeping into the beer mug. Unexpectedly, she sat on the couch beside me.

'Hi, Vardan. This is Disha,' she spoke softly, trying her best to maintain the accent. The asshole had told her my name.

You won't get any direction here, I thought. I emptied my beer mug and asked the waiter for a refill.

'You sat on my friend's seat,' I said without looking at her.

'Oh! Adithya! He is a nice guy! I just met him. He won't mind,' she exclaimed. 'I have seen you here a few times,' she added, grinning.

'He dances nice too. Why don't you join him?' I said sarcastically.

'What about you? Don't you dance?' she prattled. Her Khan Market accent was pricking my ear.

I didn't answer her. I focused back on my beer. And then she placed her hand on my left thigh and her leg rubbed against mine. It didn't give me any sensation. I turned to look at her. Half of her breasts peeped out of her deep neck dress, ready to suck any man's attention. But honestly, it didn't affect me. I wondered if I had lost my ability to orgasm. She gazed at me with lust in her eyes as if my one single move could convince her to have sex with me on that couch.

'Your friend said you're single,' she uttered, sounding orgasmic and crawling up her hand.

I caught her hand and removed it from there. She looked at me startled.

'Did you ever love someone?' I asked suddenly.

'Ummm...a few times. Why do you ask?'

'A few times,' I murmured to myself and lay back on the couch laughing.

'Yes! And broke with my last boyfriend a month ago,' she said.

I sat back. 'Why?'

'He wasn't good in bed,' she said, smirking.

'Can Niti leave for this reason? No! No! She isn't a girl like that. Also, I wasn't bad in bed. I'm sure...I wasn't,' I talked to myself.

'Have you ever broken up with someone without a reason?' I asked. I gulped the whole mug of beer in one go.

'What???' She arched her eyebrows.

'Did you say someone *I love you* in the morning and write a text saying *I hate you* in the evening? Did you leave someone all of a sudden? Without even telling the reason?' I muttered, without looking at her and peeping into the empty beer mug. Waiter came and refilled the mug.

She pulled her hair in confusion. 'What the fuck you're talking about? You sound very strange,' she stood up and gestured to leave. And then she came back, bent forward, lifted the beer mug and emptied it.

'You're a sick. That's why you're single,' she yelled and left.

Adithya came to me running. 'You spoiled the chance again?' he asked.

No one could replace Niti in my heart. Thinking about any other girl, I felt like a whore.

* * *

I drove towards home after dropping Adithya. It was around 11pm when I reached near home. I saw my father was parking his car on the ramp outside home. I stopped few steps behind and waited for him to park his car and go inside. He came out of his car. He was unable to stand properly. He was drunk. He held on the car to keep him from falling down. He moved ahead towards the door, holding the car. And then he fell on the ground.

He tried to get up, but couldn't. I felt like going and helping him get up. But, something stopped me. He tried again and fell down on his face. Then I remembered about Niti how she used to say that I should have talked to my father. I should have tried to show love to him as love can solve anything. I imagined Niti smiling in happiness, seeing me help my father get up.

I get out of my car and ran towards him. I held his hands.

'Dad, careful,' I said, calmly. It had been years I called him Dad calmly.

He turned to look at me. He took few seconds to recognize my face.

'Vardan! My only son! My son is helping me get up!' he blurted out, standing up.

'Dad, why do you drink too much?' I asked, slapping on his blazer to remove dirt.

'You hate me? You think I'm rude? You think I'm a bad father?' he mumbled instead, putting his hand on my shoulder.

'No Dad! I don't. I don't hate you. I love you,' I said and hugged him. I couldn't remember when I hugged him last time—might be in my childhood. It gave me some kind of relief. I got goose bumps. We sat on the door.

'*Beta*, I know I'm rude after a few pegs. But I have never hated you. You're my only son. Everything I do is for you only,' he said, his eyes were wet. I scolded myself for hating him my whole life.

'Niti was right,' I murmured to myself.

'Niti? Who Niti?' he asked.

'No! Nothing Dad! Let's go inside,' I said. And then I heard the door open. We turned back. My mother was standing on the door, flabbergasted to see us sitting together.

'You think I hate your mother? No! I love her very much...since the day I saw her first in college,' he uttered, ending smiling.

'Mom, come! Come for a family hug,' I said. She smiled, eyes filled with tears. Tears of happiness.

49.

After Three Years

'Easy...easy man! Don't shout at them,' I yelled at Adithya. He was trying to manage some mischievous children and shouted at few of them who weren't listening to him. One of the children thrashed Adithya's ass and ran away giggling. I laughed at Adithya's exasperated reaction.

We were at the orphanage. I, Sejal, Wimp, Adithya and his girlfriend Khushi, we all were there except the one whose birthday we were celebrating. Yes! It was Niti's birthday. I celebrated her birthday every year in the same orphanage. We came there in the morning, decorated the whole orphanage and cut the cake. There was a little girl named Niti. I made her cut the cake. Children started leaping and blasting the balloons as little Niti blew the candles off.

I cut the giant cake in pieces and Wimp put them on plates filled with chocolates and mixture, Sejal handed over the plates to the children, who stood in the queue impatiently, Khushi poured them cold drink in the disposable glasses and Adithya made sure the mischievous children don't fight and break the queue.

'I feel bad for you. And I miss Niti,' said Wimp. She said this every time we met.

I scowled at her. 'Can't you see I have a knife?' I asked, showing her the plastic knife in my hand.

'I don't mean to hurt you. I just said like that,' she uttered, putting two pieces of cake in one plate.

'These children will definitely hurt you if anyone of them won't get the cake,' I said, running the knife on cake. She removed the extra piece of cake from that plate and got back to work.

After five minutes or so, she spoke again. 'There is one thing I had to tell you...but I always forget,' she uttered.

Wimp, I will kill you if you again start talking about Niti, I thought.

'What is this about?' I asked.

'It is about Niti...I,' I cut her off before she could complete.

'Wimp, what's wrong with you. Just focus on the work. Otherwise you won't get the cake like last time,' I yelled, cutting a large piece of cake in two.

'I thought it might be important. Actually, that day I saw Niti going out of the class with Divya...five minutes before the exam ended. But it's okay,' she said. The knife in my hand froze in air. I turned to look at her.

'WHAT???' abruptly, I shouted. Everyone turned to look at us, including the children. Scared, Wimp fell down from the chair.

'Yes! She left with her...I saw her leaving with Divya,' she said, settling down, her lips shivered.

'And you're telling me this after three years??? AFTER FUCKING THREE YEARS???' I screeched at her.

'I told you I forgot. I didn't know if it was important,' she murmured.

'Bitch!' I murmured to myself.

'Please, don't abuse me. I forgot. I'm sorry!' yelped Wimp. I wasn't calling her a bitch. Divya was the one who deserved that.

I left the knife there and stood up. I washed my hands and went near Adithya.

'Bro! Please, take care of it! I'm going!' I said to Adithya.

* * *

I banged at Divya's door. Her mother answered it.

'Vardan??? How come? After a long time. And *beta*, doorbell is here,' she exclaimed, showing me the doorbell outside their door. Divya's mother knew me. I had once visited her place. Her mother liked me and my car.

'Aunty, is Divya home?' I asked instead.

'Yes, yes! She is in her room,' she said. 'Divvu, *beta*, see, who has come,' she ended in one breath.

I entered.

'I always ask her about you,' her mother uttered while I walked towards Divya's room. Her room seemed embarrassingly familiar.

She was left shocked as I pushed her room's door open. She wore a red pair of shorts and a loose t-shirt. She removed her headphones.

'HEY! YOU???' shouted Divya, gaping, eyes wide open and hands on her cheeks. She ran to hug me. I didn't move my hands. I wasn't there to hug her.

'Vardan, you need tea or coffee?' interrupted her mother. Divya released me from her grip.

'Aunty, can you leave us for a moment? I need to talk to her?' I asked her mother, gazing.

She left, moping.

'You didn't change. You're still rude,' said Divya, smiling weirdly. I wanted to put tape on her mouth. She continued, 'I made you so many calls. I texted you to catch up and go out somewhere. But you replied none. Why?' She came close to me and put her hands around my waist.

She tried calling me after college. She had been asking me to meet and go out with her for a few months continuously. Even she sent few of her half naked pictures. I didn't respond to her calls and texts. Nor I gave any heed to the pictures she sent.

'What did you say her?' I asked, ignoring all her concerns and removing her hands out of my waist.

'What??? Who?' she asked, making a confused face.

'Niti! What did you say her?'

'I don't know what you are talking about,' she said and looked away. She was lying. It was all on her face.

'Don't fuck with me. I know...that day, you left the exam hall with her,' I yelled at her. I was really dying to know what venom she had expectorated out to Niti.

'Vardan, it's been three years. She isn't even in your life. Let's forget all this and make a new start. You remember this bed? Remember the moments we shared on it?' I still smile remembering how I had stopped you before entering me,' she murmured, sounding orgasmic, trying to hug me and putting my one hand on her left butt shamelessly. I didn't want to remember that once I wanted to fuck her on her bed. I felt lucky that she stopped me before putting my thing into her. I held on her arms and moved myself two steps back.

'I'm not here for this rubbish. Please, tell me what happened that day? Please...!' I stared into her eyes, angrily.

She spoke after a few minutes of resistance.

'Fine! We met in the washroom that day. I asked her to meet me after the exam. I told her that I was going to reveal something surprising about you. She denied and asked me to tell right away. Then I said her clearly that if she doesn't meet me after the exam then she would regret her whole life. I insisted her to meet after the exam. She nodded. And I left the class few minutes before the exam ended, signaling her to come out. She followed me. Then I told her about our relationship. I told her everything. I'm sorry I lied about one thing that we never made out. I told her that we made out only twice. I also told her about few of your previous girlfriends which you had told me. She refused to believe me. Then I showed her our pictures we had clicked in your car. I wanted to see her reaction. But she didn't say anything. She just left,' she revealed. I wanted to plaster her against the wall as soon as I heard her smutty confession. The pictures she was talking about were the selfies she took with me in my car—I was in unbuttoned shirt in those pictures and she was half naked, covering her breasts with her right hand and taking the selfie with left.

How could she lie about making out with me? How could she show that picture to anyone? How? I wondered.

I scolded myself for allowing her to take those pictures. It felt like the bitch just stabbed me on my back—though she had, a long time ago. I stood like a zombie, fuming. Blood in my veins started circulating rapidly. It felt like all blood in my body had gathered near my head and my head was going to blast any moment. I started feeling unconscious. I sat on the bed to keep myself from collapsing on the floor.

I looked at her, wrathfully. She didn't have any regret on her face. She had no idea what she had done to me. I never hated anyone in my whole life like I hated her in that moment.

She sat beside me and held my hand. 'I did this to get you back. She didn't deserve you the reason she went disappeared. I deserve you more than her. I met you before her. All my friends say that I was stupid to lose you. I wasn't stupid. It's just I wasn't ready for sex at that time. It was just first semester. But I'm ready now. Just make it today! Let's make out before my Mom comes. Let's make love,' she said, trying to unbutton my shirt. Blood in my body boiled after hearing the filth she had just spitted.

'BITCH! YOU ARE SUCH A WHORE! YOU RUINED MY LIFE. YOU RUINED EVERYTHING,' abruptly, I screamed out loudly, pushing her away. I stood up and frowned at her, breathing heavily. I wanted to hold her from hair and spin around the room. Wanted to thrash her face brutally. Wanted to break every bone in her body. Wanted to pull out her hair with full force. Wanted to scratch her face with my nail. I left her room as the wounded monster within me wanted to kill her at that moment.

'What happened, *beta*?' asked her mother as I stepped out of her room. She had coffee tray in her hand. Divya's father glared at me, standing beside her mother.

'Your daughter is a slut. She wants to have sex with me without protection. I'm going to buy some condoms,' I shouted loudly and left, leaving her parents dumbfounded.

S-3, Janshatabdi Express

—Delhi to Chandigarh

As he stopped speaking, I tried to check his eyes if her was crying. But he had hung his head down, staring at his sneakers. I wished he wasn't crying as I wasn't good at consoling. I wondered if I should laugh weirdly on what he had blurted out to Divya's parents or yowl out on his heart wrenching love story or pat his shoulders on becoming a potential boyfriend as his friends wanted. Well, I chose to remain calm. I didn't allow any of the feelings to appear on my face.

'So, you came to know the reason after three years,' I uttered.

He looked up and nodded. He wasn't crying, but, his eyes were wine red. I passed him my water bottle. He gulped some water and gave it back to me.

'You can wash your face,' I said, bending forward and taking the water bottle from his hand.

'No! I'm fine,' he said, showing his hand. I had so many things hovering over my head to ask him. But, I gave him some time to relax. My legs had frozen as I was sitting cross-legged for last few hours. I opened my legs, stretching straight.

'Why didn't you tell her about all your un-suck-sex-full relationships?' after ten minutes of silence or so, I asked this question which was eating my brain more than others, smile on my face. I stood on my sensation legs. I miss-pronounced the word *unsuccessful*, remembering his thirteen short-term girlfriends before Niti, to trim down the dreariness there. Though, he didn't smile back.

'I regret about it. I live in guilt of hiding all that from her. I know I had to let her know all this. I had to let her know that how I felt about the word *love* before she came in my life. I had to let her know about my wicked idea of a successful relationship. I had to let her know how I treated girls before her. And I had to let her know how she changed my life completely. Honestly, I always thought to tell her, but when she told me the reason her mother killed herself, I couldn't dare to,' he said in a regretting voice. I sat back on my seat. I felt bad for him. Life kicked him in ass when he had stopped being an asshole.

'And when she came to know about this, she couldn't take it. She might have related her situation with her mother,' I assumed.

'Yes! She might have imagined me as a womanizer. She might have doubted my love for her. It might have broken her into pieces. I know,' he said. His eyes turned soggy. He snuffled and wiped his nose. I wanted to give him my hanky. Unfortunately, I didn't have one.

'You think she can do something like her mother?' I asked and scolded myself immediately. I felt myself stupid for asking like that. He was madly in love with her, was desperately waiting for her for years to turn back in his life, and I was asking if she killed herself like her mother.

He glowered at me straight, puckering his brows. I imagined his fist coming towards me to thrash my face maliciously. I couldn't look at his grumbling eyes. I looked away. I thought to stand up, start walking—acting like I was stretching my legs, and run away from there.

'Please, don't say this,' he protested, his voice stern. I took a sigh of relief. I dropped my idea of running away from there.

'I'm sorry. I didn't mean that.'

'She cannot do that. She cannot kill herself. I know her,' he murmured to himself.

It was stupid of me to bring this. Please forget it, I thought.

'How long it had been?' I asked, trying to change the topic of dead or alive. 'I mean for how long you have been waiting for her?'

'Ummm, it's been around five years now,' he acknowledged, smiling. I could feel the pain in his smile.

'FIVE YEARS???' I blurted out as if he had uttered fifty years.

He nodded. 'Five years of hope. Five years of pain. Five years of unrest. Five years of loving her without her physical presence in my life. And five years of flipping on her old pictures and reading our chats,' he murmured, looking outside the window, and turned to look at me. 'There wasn't even a single day that I didn't miss her. I miss her every day, every moment,' he added.

'What if she doesn't come back or you couldn't find her? Doesn't this thought bother you,' I asked a serious question. I wondered if he considered me a jinx and stopped talking to me.

'Yeah! It does. Sometimes, it does. Also, my mother and my friends—Sejal and Adithya keep asking me to move on. But, my heart doesn't allow me to think beyond her. Something inside my heart says that I will find her one day. It says that my love will win one day,' he acknowledged, his voice firm.

I looked at him with my drenched eyes. For a moment, I imagined myself in his situation. I felt a paroxysm of pain inside my nose and around my jaw. I sniffed.

'I wish it happens very soon. I really do,' I mumbled, smiling.

He smiled back in a gesture to say thanks.

'Well, what do you do except rummaging around for the love of your life? And what about your father? Did you join his business or not?' I asked laughingly. He laughed back, for the first time since he started telling me his unfinished love story.

'Things are better now. And I had started going to office with him after the day I helped him get up and we hugged. Well, he does behave rude sometimes, after a few pegs of whiskey, but I don't respond back the way I used to. I always try to be nice with him. And sometimes I sit and talk to him,' he said, grinning.

The train slowed down its speed as the next station came. It was Ambala.

'My station came,' I uttered in a depressing voice as if I didn't want the conversation to stop. It was one of the best journeys I had.

'You were so clever. You kept asking question and I couldn't know anything about you,' he smirked.

I laughed, keeping my stuff in my bag. 'I had to know it after you said *love made you look like this*. Otherwise, it could have bothered me,' I muttered, zipping up my bag. 'Well, it will still bother me...thinking that you got her back or not,' I added, puckering my face.

He grinned. 'Well, what do you do?'

'I'm studying commerce.'

'And after that?' he asked. I wondered if he was going to offer me a job in his father's company. I lifted my bag as the train stopped.

'I will start doing a job. But, I feel like I can tell some stories. It's my dream. I want to become a writer,' I acknowledged.

Then you should start writing without waiting for the right moment.'

I shook my head. I hugged him and walked towards the door.

'Will you write my story?' he shouted from behind.

I stopped at the door and turned back to look at him.

'If I could become one. But I like happy endings,' I said, smiling.

I left.

50.

After Three Years

'Thank you, sir,' said one of the beautiful readers, taking a selfie with me. I was at the launch of my debut novel *I'm An Average Looking Boy...will you be my girlfriend*? at Oxford Bookstores, Connaught Place, New Delhi. At the end of the event, I was signing books for more than hundreds of my readers who had turned up to make the event successful. After signing around fifty to sixty books, I started feeling soreness in my right hand fingers. So, I started increasing the speed of signing to finish it asap. And when the next person came with the book I tried to take it from his hand to sign it. But I couldn't as he had held it tightly. I tried one more time and realised he was in no mood of leaving the book. Startled, I looked up at him. He looked much elder than the other readers there. He wore a grey tuxedo with white shirt. He was slim, fair and tall with clean shave and well combed hair. He looked like an MNC manager. He was constantly smirking at me. Bemused, I arched my brows at him.

Is he one of those critics who troll romance authors for writing in simple English? I wondered.

I realized there was a lady standing behind him. She came forward and stood beside him, holding his hand. She wore a Saree. She was above average in looks. One of the most beautiful girls I had ever seen in my life, I must say.

Is she also a critic? I'm not going to mind if she trolls me or my book, I thought.

And then I glanced at the fancy watch that tuxedo guy was wearing. I felt like I had seen that watch somewhere. And I stared at his face carefully, puckering up my eyes.

I stood up. 'OH MY GOD!!! VARDAN???' suddenly, I shouted loudly, aghast. As loud as everyone in the bookstore could hear it. All the readers turned to look at me, startled. I trimmed down the sudden excitement on my face.

He nodded, smiling.

'And she?' I asked, looking at the gorgeous lady, standing right to him.

'Hi, I'm Niti,' she said, offering her hand. We shook hands. It felt soft. I gazed at her for a few seconds, my mouth open. I was flabbergasted, seeing them together. A sudden smile of happiness occurred on my face.

Man! She is more beautiful than you described her. Worth loving! Worth waiting! I thought to tell him.

'You're looking so different,' uttered Vardan, breaking the awkward silence there.

'Not more different than you, though,' I said, smiling. I was constantly smiling.

'Love made me look like this, one more time,' he uttered, laughingly. 'Well, sign our book and continue taking pictures with your lovely readers. We are waiting.'

'Yes! Sure,' I said. I signed their book and they sat in the last row. Then I continued with the signing. I kept smiling and squinting at the beautiful couple while signing and taking pictures with other readers.

Well, I rushed to them as soon as I ran my pen on the last reader's book and took a picture with him.

They stood up. 'So, you finally made it! You became a writer,' said Vardan.

'You also made it,' I smirked.

'Now you guys talk. I will have to take a leave,' interrupted Niti.

'She has to go somewhere. I brought her here so that she could meet an upcoming author,' explained Vardan, grinning and looking at me.

'So, I should call you author Roopesh or Roopesh sir,' she wittered, smiling.

'Don't embarrass me. Call me just Roopesh,' I said shyly.

'Okay! Okay! Sorry, Roopesh. I have to take a leave like this. Hope we meet some other day,' she said, crinkling her nose.

'It's okay! Thanks for coming, though,' I said. Well, let's get one picture first,' I added, immediately. I called my photographer. He clicked a picture of us together. And then she left.

'I'm happy for you,' said Vardan as Niti left.

'I'm happier than you, man. Tell me how, when and where it happened? How did you guys reunite? She came back or you found her? Did she call you? Did you find her at her grandparents place? At any orphanage?' I exclaimed, firing a bunch of questions at him. 'I can't wait. I'm eager to know this.' I looked at him for an immediate answer. My heart was leaping in my throat.

He laughed. My brows furrowed.

'Wait! Wait! Should I tell you right now or we can have a coffee first?' he uttered in between the laughter.

'Yes! Why not?'

We went to the Starbucks which was at a few steps of walk from the bookstore. I was in a hurry to know how they came back together. So, without making any delay, I asked him for his choice and ordered our coffee. And he started telling me the last chapter of his love story with a sip of coffee.

51.

'Why do you still hold onto it, when you know it's killing you every day?' uttered Sejal, while Adithya nodded in her support. It was after six months since we met in train. I was getting ready for my journey—in search of her. Sejal and Adithya were at my place that day, nattering the move on thing.

'Only the love of my life can save me...nothing else,' I smirked, throwing a pair of jeans in my backpack and looking at them. Sejal made a face. Then I felt someone was at the door. I turned towards the door. It was my mother. She walked inside.

'How long he will meander in trains for that girl?' asked my mother, looking at my move on experts. 'He does it almost every month. It's been more than five years now,' she added before the experts could make their comments.

'Mom, please don't start it again. I'm already late,' I muttered, lifting my bag and gesturing to leave.

'Aunty, I'm asking him to find a new girl. But, he doesn't listen to me,' interrupted Adithya.

'It scares me now. I don't know if he will marry or not.' My mother threw her hand on forehead. She stood in front of me and stared at me.

'What?' I asked her.

'Asha has told me about a girl.' Asha was my mother's elder sister. She kept suggesting my mother a new girl for me every week. And I kept rejecting without even looking at the pictures. Then my mother lied to her that I didn't like the girl. But Asha aunty wasn't ready to give up.

'So?'

'Promise me that you will meet her after you come back,' she put my hand on her head. She didn't have even one percent of expectation that I could come back with Niti. No one had. Except me.

'Mom, don't be so filmy. You know I cannot make false promises to you,' I removed my hand from her head. 'Trust me I will find her one day,' I said.

She looked away, sulking. I felt bad for disappointing her.

Well, Adithya and Sejal came to drop me to the New Delhi railway station. I got down and rushed to the station as Sejal stopped the car. I even left the car door open. I was late. I ran towards my platform. And when I reached there I saw the train was running faster than me. I ran behind the train, but couldn't match with the speed.

'Damn! I missed the train. I fucking missed it,' I murmured to myself as I stopped. I bent down, gasping loudly, hands on my knees. I was feeling bad as if I didn't miss just a train but Niti one more time.

I sat on a bench there, breathing heavily and thinking if I had to take a flight or go back to home. My throat had dried. I felt thirsty. I looked around for any shops where I could buy some water. I saw a railway food-stall there, surrounded with a few bunch of children, leaping on each other. I stood up and walked towards that stall to buy a water bottle. And as I reached near, I saw a girl on that stall. I faced her back. She was wearing a Saree. Unexpectedly, something started happening inside my veins. My heart started pumping at double speed. And I froze at a distance as she turned her side and I looked at her. I couldn't believe my eyes what I saw there. I blinked my eyes rapidly.

It felt like I was dreaming something. It was her. That girl was Niti. The girl I was in love with. The girl I have been waiting for years. The girl I have been searching everywhere for last few years. And the girl I missed the most in every breath I took. It was her.

'NITI...???' all of a sudden, I screamed out loudly, my bag fell on the floor. She was looking at me surprised. She was holding two water bottles in each her hands. Bottles fell from her hands. Abruptly, children stopped leaping. She didn't respond. She didn't move an inch. She stood there astonished.

I felt a pang near my throat. Millions of emotions were jumping in the upper floor of my body. I tried to move towards her, but couldn't as I fell on my knees. My eyes filled with tears. I had so many things to complain about. I always thought I would tell her that how much I had to go through after her sudden disappearance. But my heart collapsed as my eyes collided with hers. Now I was wondering what to say.

'Where had you gone, Niti? You know I have been waiting for you since then, every single day. There was not a single moment I didn't think about you...? I missed you a lot, baby,' I spoke loudly, on my knees. All the children there turned to look at me, surprised. I couldn't stop my tears rolling down my eyes.

And then, all of a sudden, she ran towards me. I stood up and she jumped to hug me. She started crying. There were people looking at us in the station. But we didn't care. We could see only each other. Her touch felt like water to an almost dried plant.

'I'm sorry, Vardan. I'm really sorry. I always loved you. I too missed you. I never wanted to leave you like that. I never wanted to. I didn't know how to react. I was mad at you when Divya told me something terrible about you. I couldn't take that. I cried a lot. I felt choked. It was really suffocating. I thought I would never talk to you again...' she burst out while crying in my arms. She said all that in one breath before I stopped her.

'Yes, yes! Baby I know what Divya did. And I know I should have told you all that before. But trust me I never cheated on you. I never faked my love for you. I genuinely loved you. I love you. And I will love you till my last breath,' I uttered, sobbing. We came out of each other's arms.

She lifted her head up and looked at me. 'Aren't you angry at me?' she asked.

'No. I'm just happy that you're with me now.' I wiped tears from her face.

'This is the first time I came to Delhi ever since that day and I had a feeling that we would meet. You know after few months when my anger and disappointment faded away, I felt like calling you. But, couldn't gather courage. I scolded myself for leaving like that. I felt like I should have...' I put one finger on her lips and cut her off before she could complete.

'Don't say anything. Just say you will never leave me alone now... even for a second,' I mumbled, sobbing and gazing into her eyes.

'Never,' she mumbled back.

I moved forward and placed my lips on hers. Children covered their eyes with hands. We kissed for a few seconds and got separated hearing the noise of claps. We looked around. Few people had gathered there and were clapping. We looked at each other embarrassingly and smiled.

Later, we dropped the kids at an NGO and went to Sejal's place. I had called Adithya at Sejal's place. They both were surprised and happy for us at the same time. Adithya was almost dancing in happiness. We talked for a few hours. During all the conversation, Adithya and Sejal kept telling Niti how desperately I was waiting for her and I kept holding her in my arms. Finally, the bunch of happy people got together.

'Okay! You guys talk...we are coming back in a while,' said Sejal. Adithya winked at me. They were leaving to give us some private time. We really need that. They both left.

We talked for a while. Niti told me that she had been working for an NGO in Pune. I told her how the things changed after she went. I told her that I was in good terms with my father now and had finally joined his business. She smiled at it. I kept gazing into her eyes during all the conversations we made. Suddenly, I stood up, holding her hand. She shook her head up. I helped her get up. And I placed my lips on hers as soon as we stepped inside the bedroom. We started kissing, after almost a half-decade. It felt like my thirsty soul for years was getting some water.

We, fell on the bed, kissing. 'I love you,' I said.

'Shut the door baby,' she whispered.

After few minutes of kissing and cuddling, I entered her. We made love. It felt like the first time. It felt like two abandoned souls were turning into one. The feeling was incredible. Anyways, I finally realized that every part in my body was still functional. I could still do it. I hadn't turned an impotent.

Epilogue

After One Year

Everyone had gathered around the stage when I reached there, running. I was at the Taj Hotel Delhi and got late due to traffic jam. Well, I was there to witness the pivotal and poignant moment of Vardan and Niti's lives. It was the day when they decided to give their relationship a social acknowledgment. It was the day of their engagement. Yes! They were getting engaged in front of hundreds of people.

I lifted my head up to peep at the stage. I saw Vardan and Niti were standing there, facing each other. Vardan was in Navy Blue slim fit tuxedo and Niti looked more beautiful in her light pink Lehenga.

'Did they exchange the rings? I guess I'm very late,' I talked to myself, while peeping through the crowd. Suddenly, everyone started shouting and hooting. I barged into the crowd and made some space for myself to get a clearer view. I saw few girls from both the families came on the stage and gave both of them their rings to exchange.

So, I have arrived at the right time, I thought. As I didn't know anyone there except the two love birds on the stage, I gave myself a company.

The marvelously decorated hall echoed with the sound of claps as

Niti placed the ring on Vardan's finger. I joined clapping. People were throwing rose petals on them. Cameramen were trying to capture every moment. And they both were looking into each other's eyes, smiling with coyness.

Now it was Vardan's turn to put the ring on her finger. Everyone started whooping and laughing, asking Vardan to come on his knees.

'On your knees, Vardan...on your knees...' everyone in the hall was chanting. I also chanted that in my head. And the next moment, Vardan held Niti's right hand and knelt down. They weren't even blinking. They were just looking into each other's eyes. It could have been seen in their eyes that how lucky they felt having each other. I took out my mobile and captured that very special moment.

Anyway, he put the ring on her finger, stood up, kissed on her head and they hugged. They were engaged now. I felt very happy for Vardan. I was one of them who knew everything that how much he had suffered. Well, they both sat on the royal couch there and people started coming to get clicked with the gorgeous couple. I waved at Vardan as our eyes met. He signalled me to come on the stage while smiling and faking a pose for the camera.

I showed him my hand, making him sure that it was okay and I was waiting for my turn.

'Hey.' I heard a voice coming from behind. I turned back and saw two girls looking and smiling at me. I was a little confused.

'Yes?' I said.

'You're Roopesh Kumar? Right?' one of them asked and paused to gauge my reaction.

I nodded.

'Hi, this is Sejal. Vardan told us about you,' she said, offering her hand. We shook hands.

'Oh, yes! Even he told me about you,' I said.

'Hey, I read your debut novel. I really loved Dibisha in that. I really loved the poem she wrote having tears in her eyes,' interrupted the another girl smiling continuously, looking at me. She looked like a newly married girl. 'I'm Dimple, by the way,' she added, offering her hand. When Vardan had told me about her four peeping teeth, I thought he was kidding. But he wasn't.

So, she is married now, I thought.

'Thank you so much. Glad you loved my book,' I said. We shook hands. 'And Dimple urff Wimp?'

She made a face. 'Yes! My college nick name,' uttered Wimp. Sejal laughed.

'Come with me...if you want to meet Vardan. Otherwise she will keep talking,' said Sejal, grinning.

'Sure,' I said, smiling. We walked towards the stage. Wimp followed us.

'Congratulations to the beautiful couple,' I said, shaking hands with them as I reached there. I handed over the bouquet to Niti.

'Thank you,' said Niti, smiling.

'Thanks for coming, bro,' added Vardan.

'No, formalities, boss. I would have come even if you hadn't invited me,' I smirked.

'So, you met my friends?' asked Vardan, looking at Sejal and Wimp.

'Yes, I did. Except Adithya. Where is he?'

'He is managing all this with Dad,' said Vardan and paused to look at a distance. 'Look he is there with the catering manager.'

I turned to look where he was pointing. And then Wimp shouted loudly. 'ADITHYAAAA.'

He walked towards us.

'What happened? Why are you screaming?' he said, glowering at Wimp as he reached near. Wimp hid behind Sejal.

'You remember, I had told you about someone I met on the train?' interrupted Vardan.

'Yes, who turned an author and you both went to his book launch,' answered Adithya.

'Yes. Here he is,' said Vardan, pointing at me.

'Hey, hi. Very nice to see you here,' he offered his hand, bending forward. We shook hands.

'Same here,' I said. 'Well, where is your girlfriend, Khushi?'

'You know about her?' he asked, sounding surprised.

'I know about you all,' I said, smiling and looking at Vardan. He smiled back.

'We broke up...two years ago,' he uttered.

'Why? What happened?'

'She said I didn't care about her and didn't give her the amount of time and attention she needed,' he revealed, sulking. He fell quiet.

After few seconds of silence, I said, 'Now, it's time for you to become a *POTENTIAL BOYFRIEND*.'

We all laughed together.